A
TOR
DOUBLE
ACTION
WESTERN

Look for Tor Double Action Westerns
from these authors

MAX BRAND
ZANE GREY
LEWIS B. PATTEN
WAYNE D. OVERHOLSER
CLAY FISHER
FRANK BONHAM
OWEN WISTER
STEVE FRAZEE*
HARRY SINCLAIR DRAGO*
JOHN PRESCOTT*
WILL HENRY*

*Coming soon

Owen Wister

A PILGRIM ON THE GILA
LA TINAJA BONITA

TOR

A TOM DOHERTY ASSOCIATES BOOK
NEW YORK

A PILGRIM ON THE GILA

LA TINAJA BONITA

A Tor Book
Published by Tom Doherty Associates, Inc.
49 West 24th Street
New York, N.Y. 10010

Cover art by Bernal

ISBN: 0-812-50887-4

First Tor edition: August 1990

Printed in the United States of America

0 9 8 7 6 5 4 3 2 1

A Pilgrim on the Gila

CHAPTER I

Midway from Grant to Thomas comes Pay-master's Hill, not much after Cedar Springs and not long before you sight the valley where the Gila flows. This lonely piece of road must lie three thousand miles from Washington; but in the holiday journey that I made they are near together among the adventures of mind and body that overtook me. For as I turned southward our capital was my first stopping-place, and it was here I gathered the expectations of Arizona with which I continued on my way.

Arizona was the unknown country I had chosen for my holiday, and I found them describing it in our National House of Rep-resentatives, where I had strolled for sight-seeing but stayed to listen. The Democrats were hot to make the Territory a State, while the Republicans objected that the place had about it still too much of the raw frontier. The talk and replies of each party were not long in shaking off restraint, and in the sharp exchange of satire the Republicans were reminded that they had not thought Idaho and Wyoming unripe at a season when those Territories were rumored to be Republican. Arizona might be Democratic, but neither cattle wars nor mine revolutions flourished there. Good order and prosperity prevailed. A member from Pennsylvania presently lost his temper, declaring that gigantic generalities about milk and honey and enlightenment would not avail to change his opinion. Arizona was well on to three times the size of New York—had a hundred and thirteen thousand square miles. Square miles of what? The desert of Sahara was twice as big as Arizona, and one of the largest misfortunes on the face of the earth. Arizona had sixty thousand inhabitants, not quite so many as the town of Troy. And what sort of people? He understood that cactus was Arizona's chief crop, stage-robbing her most active industry, and the Apache her leading citizen.

And then the Boy Orator of the Rio Grande took his good chance. I forgot his sallow face and black, unpleasant hair, and even his single gesture—that straining lift of one hand above the shoulder during the suspense of a sentence and that cracking it down into the other at the full stop, endless as a pile-driver. His facts wiped any trick of manner from my notice. Indians? Stage-robbers? Cactus? Yes. He would add famine, drought, impotent law, daily murder; he could add much more, but it was all told in Mr. Pumpelly's book, true as life, thirty years ago—doubtless the latest news in Pennsylvania! Had this report discouraged the gentleman from visiting Arizona? Why, he could go there to-day in a Pullman car by two great roads and eat his three meals in security. But Eastern statesmen were too often content with knowing their particular corner of our map while a continent of ignorance lay in their minds.

At this stroke applause sounded beside me, and, turning, I had my first sight of the yellow duster. The bulky man that wore it shrewdly and smilingly watched the orator, who now dwelt upon the rapid benefits of the railways, the excellent men and things they brought to Arizona, the leap into civilization that the Territory had taken. "Let Pennsylvania see those blossoming fields for herself," said he, "those boundless contiguities of shade." And a sort of cluck went off down inside my neighbor's throat, while the speaker with rising heat gave us the tonnage of plums exported from the Territory during the past fiscal year. Wool followed.

"Sock it to 'em, Limber Jim!" murmured the man in the duster, and executed a sort of step. He was plainly a personal acquaintance of the speaker's.

Figures never stick by me, nor can I quote accurately the catalogue of statistic abundance now recited in the House of Representatives; but as wheat, corn, peaches, apricots, oranges, raisins, spices, the rose and the jasmine flowered in the Boy Orator's eloquence, the genial antics of my neighbor increased until he broke into delighted mutterings, such as "He's a studhorse," and "Put the kybosh on 'em," and many more that have escaped my memory. But the Boy Orator's peroration I am glad to remember, for his fervid convictions lifted him into the domain of metaphor and cadence; and though to be sure I made due allowance for enthusiasm, his picture of Arizona remained vivid with me, and I should have voted to make the Territory a State that very day.

"With her snow-clad summits, with the balm of her Southern vineyards, she loudly calls for a sister's rights. Not the isles of Greece, nor any cycle of Cathay, can compete with her horticultural resources, her

Salt River, her Colorado, her San Pedro, her Gila, her hundred irrigated valleys, each one surpassing the shaded Paradise of the Nile, where thousands of noble men and elegantly educated ladies have already located, and to which thousands more, like patient monuments, are waiting breathless to throng when the franchise is proclaimed. And if my death could buy that franchise, I would joyfully boast such martyrdom."

The orator cracked his hands together in this supreme moment, and the bulky gentleman in the duster drove an elbow against my side, whispering to me at the same time behind his hand, in a hoarse confidence: "Deserted Jericho! California only holds the record on stoves now."

"I'm afraid I do not catch your allusion," I began. But at my voice he turned sharply, and, giving me one short, ugly stare, was looking about him, evidently at some loss, when a man at his farther side pulled at his duster, and I then saw that he had all along been taking me for a younger companion he had come in with, and with whom he now went away. In the jostle we had shifted places while his eyes were upon the various speakers, and to him I seemed an eavesdropper. Both he and his friend had a curious appearance, and they looked behind them, meeting my gaze as I watched them going; and then they made to each other

7

some laughing comment, of which I felt myself to be the inspiration. I was standing absently on the same spot, still in a mild puzzle over California and the record on stoves. Certainly I had overheard none of their secrets, if they had any; I could not even guess what might be their true opinion about admitting Arizona to our Union.

CHAPTER II

With this last memory of our Capitol and the statesmen we have collected there to govern us, I entered upon my holiday, glad that it was to be passed in such a region of enchantment. For peaches it would be too early, and with roses and jasmine I did not importantly concern myself, thinking of them only as a pleasant sight by the way. But on my gradual journey through Lexington, Bowling Green, Little Rock, and Fort Worth I dwelt upon the shade of the valleys, and the pasture hills dotted with the sheep of whose wool the Boy Orator had spoken; and I wished that our cold Northwest could have been given such a bountiful climate. Upon the final morning of railroad I looked out of the window at an earth which during the night had collapsed into a vacuum, as I had so often seen happen before upon more Northern parallels. The evenness of this huge nothing was cut by our track's interminable scar, and broken to the eye by the towns which now and again rose and littered the horizon like boxes dumped by emigrants. We were still in Texas, not distant from the Rio Grande, and I looked at the boxes drifting by, and wondered from which of them the Boy Orator had been let loose. Twice or three times upon this day of sand I saw green spots shining sudden and bright and Biblical in the wilderness. Their isolated loveliness was herald of the valley land I was nearing each hour. The wandering Mexicans, too, bright in rags and swarthy in nakedness, put me somehow in mind of the Old Testament.

In the evening I sat at whiskey with my first acquaintance, a Mr. Mowry, one of several Arizona citizens whom my military friend at San Carlos had written me to look out for on my way to visit him. My train had trundled on to the Pacific, and I sat in a house once more—a saloon on the platform, with an open door through which the night air came pleasantly. This was now the long-expected Territory, and time for roses and jasmine to begin. Early in our talk I naturally spoke to Mr. Mowry of Arizona's resources and her chance of becoming a State.

"We'd have got there by now," said he, "only Luke Jenks ain't half that interested in Arizona as he is in Luke Jenks."

I reminded Mr. Mowry that I was a stranger here and unacquainted with the prominent people.

"Well, Luke's as near a hog as you kin be and wear pants. Be with you in a minute," added Mr. Mowry, and shambled from the room. This was because a shot had been fired in a house across the railroad tracks. "I run two places," he explained, returning quite soon from the house and taking up the thread of his whiskey where he had dropped it. "Two outfits. This side for toorists. Th' other pays better. I come here in 'sixty-two."

"I trust no one has been—hurt?" said I, inclining my head towards the farther side of the railroad.

"Hurt?" My question for the moment conveyed nothing to him, and he repeated the word, blinking with red eyes at me over the rim of his lifted glass. "No, nobody's hurt. I've been here a long while, and seen them as was hurt, though." Here he nodded at me depreciatingly, and I felt how short was the time that I had been here. "Th' other side pays better," he resumed, "as

11

toorists mostly go to bed early. Six bits is about the figger you can reckon they'll spend, if you know anything." He nodded again, more solemn over his whiskey. "That kind's no help to business. I've been in this Territory from the start, and Arizona ain't what it was. Them mountains are named from me." And he pointed out of the door. "Mowry's Peak. On the map." With this last august statement his mind seemed to fade from the conversation, and he struck a succession of matches along the table and various parts of his person.

"Has Mr. Jenks been in the Territory long?" I suggested, feeling the silence weigh upon me.

"Luke? He's a hog. Him the people's choice! But the people of Arizona ain't what they was. Are you interested in silver?"

"Yes," I answered, meaning the political question. But before I could say what I meant he had revived into a vigor of attitude and a wakefulness of eye of which I had not hitherto supposed him capable.

"You come here," said he; and, catching my arm, he took me out of the door and along the track in the night, and round the corner of the railroad hotel into view of more mountains that lay to the south. "You stay here to-morrow," he pursued, swiftly, "and I'll hitch up and drive you over there. I'll show you some rock behind Helen's

Dome that'll beat any you've struck in the whole course of your life. It's on the wood reservation, and when the government abandons the Post, as they're going to do—"

There is no need for my entering at length into his urgence, or the plans he put to me for our becoming partners, or for my buying him out and employing him on a salary, or buying him out and employing some other, or no one, according as I chose—the whole bright array of costumes in which he presented to me the chance of making my fortune at a stroke. I think that from my answers he gathered presently a discouraging but perfectly false impression. My Eastern hat and inexperienced face (I was certainly young enough to have been his grandchild) had a little misled him; and although he did not in the least believe the simple truth I told him, that I had come to Arizona on no sort of business, but for the pleasure of seeing the country, he now overrated my brains as greatly as he had in the beginning despised them, quite persuaded I was playing some game deeper than common, and either owned already or had my eye upon other silver mines.

"Pleasure of seeing the country, ye say?" His small wet eyes blinked as he stood on the railroad track bareheaded, considering me from head to foot. "All right. Did ye say ye're going to Globe?"

"No. To San Carlos to visit an army officer."

"Carlos is on the straight road to Globe," said Mr. Mowry, vindictively. "But ye might as well drop any idea of Globe, if ye should get one. If it's copper ye're after, there's parties in ahead of you."

Desiring, if possible, to shift his mind from its present unfavorable turn, I asked him if Mr. Adams did not live between here and Solomonsville, my route to Carlos. Mr. Adams was another character of whom my host had written me, and at my mention of his name the face of Mr. Mowry immediately soured into the same expression it had taken when he spoke of the degraded Jenks.

"So you're acquainted with him! He's got mines. I've seen 'em. If you represent any Eastern parties, tell 'em not to drop their dollars down old Adams's hole in the ground. He ain't the inexperienced juniper he looks. Him and me's been acquainted these thirty years. People claim it was Cyclone Bill held up the Ehrenberg stage. Well, I guess I'll be seeing how the boys are getting along."

With that he moved away. A loud disturbance of chairs and broken glass had set up in the house across the railroad, and I watched the proprietor shamble from me with his deliberate gait towards the establishment that paid him best. He had left me possessor of much incomplete knowledge, and I waited for him, pacing the platform; but he did not return, and as I judged it inexpedient to follow him, I went to my bed on the tourist side of the track.

In the morning the stage went early, and as our road seemed to promise but little variety—I could see nothing but an empty plain—I was glad to find my single fellow-passenger a man inclined to talk. I did not like his mustache, which was too large for his face, nor his too careful civility and arrangement of words; but he was genial to excess, and thoughtful of my comfort.

"I beg you will not allow my valise to incommode you," was one of his first remarks; and I liked this consideration better than any Mr. Mowry had shown me. "I fear you will detect much initial primitiveness in our methods of transportation," he said.

This again called for gracious assurances on my part, and for a while our polite phrases balanced to corners until I was mentally winded keeping up such a pace of manners. The train had just brought him from Tucson, he told me, and would I indulge? On this we shared and complimented each other's whiskey.

"From your flask I take it that you are a Gentile," said he, smiling.

"If you mean tenderfoot," said I, "let me confess at once that flask and owner are from the East, and brand-new in Arizona."

"I mean you're not a Mormon. Most strangers to me up this way are. But they carry their liquor in a plain flat bottle like this."

"Are you a—a—" Embarrassment took me as it would were I to check myself on the verge of asking a courteously disposed stranger if he had ever embezzled.

"Oh, I'm no Mormon," my new friend said, with a chuckle, and I was glad to hear him come down to reasonable English. "But Gentiles are in the minority in this valley."

"I didn't know we'd got to the valleys yet," said I, eagerly, connecting Mormons with fertility and jasmine. And I lifted the flaps of the stage, first one side and then the other, and saw the desert everywhere flat, treeless, and staring like an eye without a lid.

"This is the San Simon Valley we've been in all the time," he replied. "It goes from Mexico to the Gila, about a hundred and fifty miles."

"Like this?"

"South it's rockier. Better put the flap down."

"I don't see where people live," I said, as two smoky spouts of sand jetted from the tires and strewed over our shoes and per-

16

vaded our nostrils. "There's nothing—yes, there's one bush coming." I fastened the flaps.

"That's Seven-Mile Mesquite. They held up the stage at this point last October. But they made a mistake in the day. The money had gone down the afternoon before, and they only got about a hundred."

"I suppose it was Mormons who robbed the stage?"

"Don't talk quite so loud," the stranger said, laughing. "The driver's one of them."

"A Mormon or a robber?"

"Well, we only know he's a Mormon."

"He doesn't look twenty. Has he many wives yet?"

"Oh, they keep that thing very quiet in these days, if they do it at all. The government made things too hot altogether. The Bishop here knows what hiding for polygamy means."

"Bishop who?"

"Meakum," I thought he answered me, but was not sure in the rattle of the stage, and twice made him repeat it, putting my hand to my ear at last. "Meakum! Meakum!" he shouted.

"Yes, sir," said the driver.

"Have some whiskey?" said my friend, promptly; and when that was over and the flat bottle passed back, he explained in a lower voice, "A son of the Bishop's."

"Indeed!" I exclaimed.

"So was the young fellow who put in the mail-bags, and that yellow-headed duck in the store this morning." My companion, in the pleasure of teaching new things to a stranger, stretched his legs on the front seat, lifted my coat out of his way, and left all formality of speech and deportment. "And so's the driver you'll have to-morrow if you're going beyond Thomas, and the stock-tender at the sub-agency where you'll breakfast. He's a yellow-head too. The old man's postmaster, and owns this stage-line. One of his boys has the mail contract. The old man runs the hotel at Solomonsville and two stores at Bowie and Globe, and the store and mill at Thacher. He supplies the military posts in this district with hay and wood, and a lot of things on and off through the year. Can't write his own name. Signs government contracts with his mark. He's sixty-four, and he's had eight wives. Last summer he married number nine—rest all dead, he says, and I guess that's so. He has fifty-seven recorded children, not counting the twins born last week. Any yellow-heads you'll see in the valley 'll answer to the name of Meakum as a rule, and the other type's curly black like this little driver specimen."

"How interesting there should be only two varieties of Meakum!" said I.

"Yes, it's interesting. Of course the whole

fifty-seven don't class up yellow or black curly, but if you could take account of stock you'd find the big half of 'em do. Mothers don't seem to have influenced the type appreciably. His eight families, successive and simultaneous, cover a period of forty-three years, and yellow and black keeps turning up right along. Scientifically, the suppression of Mormonism is a loss to the student of heredity. Some of the children are dead. Get killed now and then, and die too—die from sickness. But you'll easily notice Meakums as you go up the valley. Old man sees all get good jobs as soon as they're old enough. Places 'em on the railroad, places 'em in town, all over the lot. Some don't stay; you couldn't expect the whole fifty-seven to be steady; but he starts 'em all fair. We have six in Tucson now, or five, maybe. Old man's a good father."

"They're not all boys?"

"Certainly not; but more than half are."

"And you say he can't write?"

"Or read, except print, and he has to spell out that."

"But, my goodness, he's postmaster!"

"What's that got to do with it? Young Meakums all read like anything. He don't do any drudgery."

"Well, you wouldn't catch me signing any contracts I couldn't read."

"Do you think you'd catch anybody reading a contract wrong to old Meakum? Oh, momma! Why, he's king round here. Fixes the county elections and the price of tomatoes. Do you suppose any Tucson jury 'll convict any of his Mormons if he says nay? No, sir! It's been tried. Why, that man ought to be in Congress."

"If he's like that I don't consider him desirable," said I.

"Yes, he is desirable," said my friend, roughly. "Smart, can't be fooled, and looks after his people's interests. I'd like to know if that don't fill the bill?"

"If he defeats justice—"

"Oh, rats!" This interruption made me regret his earlier manner, and I was sorry the polish had rubbed through so quickly and brought us to a too precipitate familiarity. "We're Western out here," he continued, "and we're practical. When we want a thing, we go after it. Bishop Meakum worked his way down here from Utah through desert and starvation, mostly afoot, for a thousand miles, and his flock to-day is about the only class in the Territory that knows what prosperity feels like, and his laws are about the only laws folks don't care to break. He's got a brain. If he weren't against Arizona's being admitted—"

"He should know better than that," said I, wishing to be friendly. "With your fruit exports and high grade of citizens you'll soon be another California."

He gave me an odd look.

"I am surprised," I proceeded, amiably, "to hear you speak of Mormons only as prosperous. They think better of you in Washington."

"Now, see here," said he, "I've been pleasant to you and I've enjoyed this ride. But I like plain talk."

"What's the matter?" I asked.

"And I don't care for Eastern sarcasm."

"There was no intention—"

"I don't take offence where offence is not intended. As for high-grade citizens, we don't claim to know as much as— I suppose it's New York you come from? Gold-bugs and mugwumps—"

"If you can spare the time," said I, "and kindly explain what has disturbed you in my remarks, we'll each be likely to find the rest of these forty miles more supportable."

"I guess I can stand it," said he, swallowing a drink. He folded his arms and resettled his legs; and the noisome hatefulness of his laugh filled me with regret for the wet-eyed Mowry. I would now gladly have taken any amount of Mowry in exchange for this; and it struck me afresh how uncertainly one always reckons with those who suspect their own standing.

"Till Solomonsville," said I, "let us veil our estimation of each other. Once out of this stage and the world will be large enough for both of us." I was wrong there; but presentiments do not come to me often. So I, too, drank some of my own whiskey, lighted a cigar, and observed with pleasure that my words had enraged him.

CHAPTER III

Before either of us had devised our next remark, the stage pulled up to change horses at the first and last water in forty miles. This station was kept by Mr. Adams, and I jumped out to see the man Mr. Mowry had warned me was not an inexperienced juniper. His appearance would have drawn few but missionaries to him, and I should think would have been warning enough to any but an over-trustful child of six.

"Are you the geologist?" he said at once, coughing heavily; and when I told him I was simply enjoying a holiday, he looked at me sharply and spat against the corner of the stable. "There's one of them fellers expected," he continued, in a tone as if I need not attempt to deny that, and I felt his eye watching for signs of geology about me. I told him that I imagined the geologist must do an active business in Arizona.

"I don't hire 'em!" he exclaimed. "They can't tell me nothing about mineral."

"I suppose you have been here a long while, Mr. Adams?"

"There's just three living that come in ahead of—" The cough split his last word in pieces.

"Mr. Mowry was saying last night—"

"You've seen that old scamp, have you? Buy his mine behind Helen's Dome?"

My mirth at this turned him instantly confidential, and rooted his conviction that I was a geologist. "That's right!" said he, tapping my arm. "Don't you let 'em fool you. I guess you know your business. Now, if you want to look at good paying rock, thousands in sight, in sight, mind you—"

"Are you coming along with us?" called the little Meakum driver, and I turned and saw the new team was harnessed and he ready on his box, with the reins in his hands. So I was obliged to hasten from the disappointed Adams and climb back in my seat. The last I saw of him he was standing quite still in the welter of stable muck, stooping to his cough, the desert sun beating on his old body, and the desert wind slowly turning the windmill above the shadeless mud hovel in which he lived alone.

"Poor old devil!" said I to my enemy, half forgetting our terms in my contemplation of Adams. "Is he a Mormon?"

My enemy's temper seemed a little improved. "He's tried most everything except jail," he answered, his voice still harsh. "You needn't invest your sentiment there. He used to hang out at Twenty Mile in Old Camp Grant days, and he'd slit your throat for fifty cents."

But my sentiment was invested somehow. The years of the old-timers were ending so gray. Their heyday, and carousals, and happy-go-luckiness all gone, and in the remaining hours—what? Empty youth is such a grand easy thing, and empty age so grim!

"Has Mowry tried everything, too?" I asked.

"Including jail," said my companion; and gave me many entertaining incidents of Mowry's career with an ill-smelling saloon cleverness that put him once more into favorable humor with me, while I retained my opinion of him. "And that uneducated sot," he concluded, "that hobo with his record of cattle-stealing and claim-jumping, and his acquittal from jail through railroad influence, actually undertook to run against me last elections. My name is Jenks; Luke

Jenks, Territorial Delegate from Arizona."
He handed me his card.

"I'm just from Washington," said I.

"Well, I've not been there this session.
Important law business has detained me
here. Yes, they backed Mowry in that elec-
tion. The old spittoon had quite a following,
but he hadn't the cash. That gives you some
idea of the low standards I have to combat.
But I hadn't to spend much. This Territory's so poor they come cheap. Seventy-five
cents a head for all the votes I wanted in
Bisbee, Nogales, and Yuma; and up here the
Bishop was my good friend. Holding office
booms my business some, and that's why I
took it, of course. But I've had low standards to fight."

The Territorial Delegate now talked
freely of Arizona's frontier life. "It's all
dead," he said, forgetting in his fluency
what he had told me about Seven-Mile Mesquite and last October. "We have a com-
munity as high toned as any in the land.
Our monumental activity—" And here he
went off like a cuckoo clock, or the Boy Orator, reciting the glories of Phoenix and Salt
River, and the future of silver, in that spe-
cial dialect of platitudes which is spoken by
our more talkative statesmen, and is not
quite Latin, quite grammar, or quite falsehood. "We're not all Mowrys and Adamses,"
said he, landing from his flight.

"In a population of fifty-nine thousand," said I, heartily, "a stranger is bound to meet decent people if he keeps on."

Again he misinterpreted me, but this time the other way, bowing like one who acknowledges a compliment; and we came to Solomonsville in such peace that he would have been astonished at my private thoughts. For I had met no undisguised vagabond nor out-and-out tramp whom I did not prefer to Luke Jenks, vote-buyer and politician. With his catch-penny plausibility, his thin-spread good-fellowship, and his New York clothes, he mistook himself for a respectable man, and I was glad to be done with him.

I could have reached Thomas that evening, but after our noon dinner let the stage go on, and delayed a night for the sake of seeing the Bishop hold service next day, which was Sunday, some few miles down the valley. I was curious to learn the Mormon ritual and what might be the doctrines that such a man as the Bishop would expound. It dashed me a little to find this would cost me forty-eight hours of Solomonsville, no Sunday stage running. But one friendly English-speaking family—the town was chiefly Mexican—made some of my hours pleasant, and others I spent in walking. Though I went early to bed I slept so late that the ritual was well advanced when I reached the Mormon gathering.

From where I was obliged to stand I could only hear the preacher, already in the middle of his discourse.

"Don't empty your swill in the door-yard, but feed it to your hogs," he was saying; and any one who knows how plainly a man is revealed in his voice could have felt instantly, as I did, that here was undoubtedly a leader of men. "Rotten meat, rotten corn, spoiled milk, the truck that thoughtless folks throw away, should be used. Their usefulness has not ceased because they're rotten. That's the error of the ignorant, who know not that nothing is meant to be wasted in this world. The ignorant stay poor because they break the law of the Lord. Waste not, want not. The children of the Gentiles play in the door-yard and grow sickly and die. The mother working in the house has a pale face and poison in her blood. She cannot be a strong wife. She cannot bear strong sons to the man. He stays healthy because he toils in the field. He does not breathe the tainted air rising from the swill in the door-yard. Swill is bad for us, but it is good for swine. Waste it by the threshold it becomes deadly, and a curse falls upon the house. The mother and children are sick because she has broken a law of the Lord. Do not let me see this sin when I come among you in the valley. Fifty yards behind each house, with clean air between, let me see the well-fed swine receiving each day, as was intended, the garbage left by man. And let me see flowers in the dooryard, and stout, blooming children. We will sing the twenty-ninth hymn."

The scales had many hours ago dropped from my eyes, and I saw Arizona clear, and felt no repining for roses and jasmine. They had been a politician's way of foisting one more silver State upon our Senate, and I willingly renounced them for the real thing I was getting; for my holiday already far outspangled the motliest dream that ever visited me, and I settled down to it as we settle down in our theatre chairs, well pleased with the flying pantomime. And when, after the hymn and a blessing—the hymn was poor stuff about wanting to be a Mormon and with the Mormons stand—I saw the Bishop get into a wagon, put on a yellow duster, and drive quickly away, no surprise struck me at all. I merely said to myself: Certainly. How dull not to have foreseen that! And I knew that we should speak together soon, and he would tell me why California only held the record on stoves.

But oh, my friends, what a country we live in, and what an age, that the same stars and stripes should simultaneously wave over this and over Delmonico's! This too I kept thinking as I killed more hours in walking the neighborhood of Solomonsville, an object of more false hope to natives whom I did not then observe. I avoided Jenks, who had business clients in the town. I went among the ditches and the fields thus turned green by the channelled Gila; and though it was scarce a paradise surpassing the Nile, it was grassy and full of sweet smells until after a few miles each way, when the desert suddenly met the pleasant verdure full in the face and corroded it to death like vitriol. The sermon came back to me as I passed the little Mormon homes, and the bishop rose and rose in my esteem, though not as one of the children of light. That sagacious patriarch told his flock the things of week-day wisdom down to their level, the cleanly things next to godliness, to keep them from the million squalors that stain our Gentile poor; and if he did not sound much like the Gospel, he and Deuteronomy were alike as two peas. With him and Moses thus in my thoughts, I came back after sunset, and was gratified to be late for supper. Jenks had left the dining-room, and I ate in my own company, which had become lively and full of intelligent impressions. These I sat recording later in my journal, when a hesitating knock came at my bedroom, and two young men in cowboy costume entered like shy children, endeavoring to step without creaking.

"Meakums!" my delighted mind exclaimed, inwardly; but the yellow one introduced the black curly one as Mr. Follet, who, in turn, made his friend Mr. Cunningham known to me, and at my cordial suggestion they sat down with increasing awkwardness, first leaving their hats outside the door.

"We seen you walking around," said one.

"Lookin' the country over," said the other.

"Fine weather for travelling," said the first.

"Dusty though," said the second.

Perceiving them to need my help in coming to their point, I said, "And now about your silver mine."

"You've called the turn on us!" exclaimed yellow, and black curly slapped his knee. Both of them sat looking at me, laughing enthusiastically, and I gathered they had been having whiskey this Sunday night. I confess that I offered them some more, and when they realized my mildness they told me with length and confidence about the claims they had staked out on Mount Turnbull. "And there's lots of lead, too," said yellow.

"I do not smelt," said I, "or deal in any way with ore. I have come here without the intention of buying anything."

"You ain't the paymaster?" burst out

black curly, wrinkling his forehead like a pleasant dog.

Yellow touched his foot.

"Course he ain't!" said curly, with a swerve of his eye. "He ain't due. What a while it always is waitin'!"

Now the paymaster was nothing to me, nor whom he paid. For all I knew, my visitors were on his roll; and why yellow should shy at the mention of him and closely watch his tipsy mate I did not try to guess. Like every one I had met so far in Arizona, these two evidently doubted I was here for my pleasure merely; but it was with entire good-humor that they remarked a man had the right to mind his own business; and so, with a little more whiskey, we made a friendly parting. They recommended me to travel with a pistol in this country, and I explained that I should do myself more harm than good with a weapon that any one handled more rapidly than I, with my inexperience.

"Good-night, Mr. Meakum," I said.

"Follet," corrected black curly.

"Cunningham," said yellow, and they picked up their hats in the hall and withdrew.

I think now those were their names—the time was coming when I should hear them take oath on it—yet I do not know. I heard many curious oaths taken.

CHAPTER IV

I was glad to see black curly in the stage
next day, not alone for his company, but to
give him a right notion of what ready money
I had about me. Thinking him over, and his
absence of visible means of support, and his
interest in me, I took opportunity to mention, quite by the way, that five or six dollars was all that I ever carried on my
person, the rest being in New York drafts,
worthless in any hands but mine. And I
looked at the time once or twice for him to
perceive the cheapness of my nickel watch.
That the Bishop was not his father I had
indirect evidence when we stopped at
Thacher to change horses and drop a mail-
sack, and the Mormon divine suddenly

lifted the flap and inspected us. He nodded to me and gave Follet a message.

"Tell your brother" (wouldn't a father have said Tom or Dick?) "that I've given him chances enough and he don't take 'em. He don't feed my horses, and my passengers complain he don't feed them—though that's not so serious!" said he to me, with a jovial wink. "But I won't have my stock starved. You'll skip the station and go through to Thomas with this pair," he added to the driver in his voice of lusty command. "You'll get supper at Thomas. Everything's moved on there from to-day. That's the rule now." Then he returned to black curly, who, like the driver, had remained cowed and respectful throughout the short harangue. "Your brother could have treated me square and made money by that station. Tell him that, and to see me by Thursday. If he's thinking of peddling vegetables this season I'll let him sell to Fort Bowie. Safford takes Carlos, and I won't have two compete in the same market, or we'll be sinking low as Eastern prices," said he to me, with another wink. "Drive on now. You're late."

He shut the flap, and we were off quickly—too quickly. In the next few moments I could feel that something all wrong went on; there was a jingle and snapping of harness, and such a voice from the Bishop behind us that I looked out to see him. We had stopped, and he was running after us at a wonderful pace for a man of sixty-four.

"If you don't drive better than that," said the grizzled athlete, arriving cool and competent, "you'll saw wood for another year. Look how you've got them trembling."

It was a young pair, and they stood and steamed while the broken gear was mended.

"What did California hold the record in before the Boy Orator broke it?" said I, getting out.

He shot at me the same sinister look I had seen in the Capitol, the look he must always wear, I suppose, when taken aback. Then he laughed broadly and heartily, a strong pleasant laugh that nearly made me like him. "So you're that fellow! Ho, ho! Away down here now. Oh, ho, ho! What's your business?"

"You wouldn't believe if I told you," said I, to his sudden sharp question.

"Me? Why, I believe everything I'm told. What's your name?"

"Will you believe I haven't come to buy anybody's silver mine?"

"Silver! I don't keep it. Unloaded ten years ago before the rabbit died."

"Then you're the first anti-silver man I've met."

"I'm anti anything I can't sell, young man. Here's all there is to silver: Once upon a time it was hard to get, and we had to have it. Now it's easy. When it gets as common as dirt it'll be as cheap as dirt. Same as watermelons when it's a big crop. D'you follow me? That's silver for you, and I don't want it. So you've come away down here. Well, well! What did you say your name was?"

I told him.

"Politician?"

"God forbid!"

"Oh, ho, ho! Well, yes. I took a look at those buzzards there in Washington. Our Senate and Representatives. They were screeching a heap. All about ratios. You'll be sawing wood yet!" he shouted to the driver, and strode up to help him back a horse. "Now ratio is a good-sounding word too, and I guess that's why they chew on it so constant. Better line of language that they get at home. I'll tell you about Congress. Here's all there is to it: You can divide them birds in two lots. Those who know better and those who don't. D'you follow me?"

"And which kind is the Boy Orator?"

"Limber Jim? Oh, he knows better. I know Jim. You see, we used to have a saying in Salt Lake that California had the smallest stoves and the biggest liars in the world. Now Jim—well, there's an old saying busted. But you'll see Arizona 'll go back

36

on the Democrats. If they put wool on the free list she'll stay Republican, and they won't want her admitted, which suits me first-rate. My people here are better off as they stand.''

"But your friend Mr. Jenks favors admission!" I exclaimed.

"Luke? He's been talking to you, has he? Well now, Luke. Here's all there is to him: Natural gas. That's why I support him, you see. If we sent a real smart man to Washington he might get us made a State. Ho, ho! But Luke stays here most of the time, and he's no good anyway. Oh, ho, ho! So you're buying no mines this season?''

Once more I found myself narrating the insignificance of my visit to Arizona—the Bishop must have been a hard inquisitor for even the deeply skilful to elude—and for the first time my word was believed. He quickly took my measure, saw that I had nothing to hide, and after telling me I could find good hunting and scenery in the mountains north, paid me no further attention, but masterfully laid some final commands on the intimidated driver. Then I bade goodbye to the Bishop, and watched that old locomotive moving vigorously back along the road to his manifold business.

The driver was ill pleased to go hungry for his supper until Thomas, but he did not dare complain much over the new rule, even to black curly and me. This and one other thing impressed me. Some miles farther on we had passed out of the dust for a while, and rolled up the flaps.

"She's waiting for you," said the driver to black curly, and that many-sided youth instantly dived to the bottom of the stage, his boots and pistol among my legs.

"Throw your coat over me," he urged.

I concealed him with that and a mail-sack, and stretched my head out to see what lioness stood in his path. But it was only a homelike little cabin, and at the door a woman, comely and mature, eying the stage expectantly. Possibly wife, I thought, more likely mother, and I asked, "Is Mrs. Follet strict?" choosing a name to fit either.

The driver choked and chirruped, but no sound came from under the mail-sack until we had passed the good-day to the momentous female, whose response was harsh with displeasure as she wheeled into her door. A sulky voice then said, "Tell me when she's gone, Bill." But we were a safe two hundred yards on the road before he would lift his head, and his spirits were darkened during the remainder of the journey.

"Come and live East," said I, inviting him to some whiskey at the same time. "Back there they don't begin sitting up for you so early in the evening."

This did not enliven him, although upon

our driver it seemed to bring another fit as much beyond the proportion of my joke as his first had been. "She tires a man's spirit," said black curly, and with this rueful utterance he abandoned the subject; so that when we reached Thomas in the dim night my curiosity was strong, and I paid little heed to this new place where I had come or to my supper. Black curly had taken himself off, and the driver sat at the table with me, still occasionally snickering in his plate. He would explain nothing that I asked him until the gaunt woman who waited on us left us for the kitchen, when he said, with a nervous, hasty relish, "The Widow Sproud is slick," and departed.

Consoled by no better clew than this I went to bed in a down-stairs room, and in my strange rising next day I did not see the driver again. Callings in the air awaked me, and a wandering sound of wheels. The gaunt woman stood with a lamp in my room saying the stage was ready, and disappeared. I sprang up blindly, and again the callings passed in the blackness outside— long cries, inarticulate to me. Wheels heavily rolled to my door, and a whip was struck against it, and there loomed the stage, and I made out the calling. It was the three drivers, about to separate before the dawn on their three diverging ways, and they were wailing their departure through the town that travellers might hear, in whatever place they lay sleeping. "Boo-wie! All aboa-rd!" came from somewhere, dreary and wavering, met at farther distance by the floating antiphonal, "Aboa-rd, aboa-rd for Grant!" and in the chill black air my driver lifted his portion of the strain, chanting, "Car-los! Car-los!" One last time he circled in the nearer darkness with his stage to let me dress. Mostly unbuttoned, and with not even a half minute to splash cold water in my eyes, I clambered solitary into the vehicle and sat among the leather mail-bags, some boxes, and a sack of grain, having four hours yet till breakfast for my contemplation. I heard the faint reveille at Camp Thomas, but to me it was a call for more bed, and I pushed and pulled the grain-sack until I was able to distribute myself and in a manner doze, shivering in my overcoat. Not the rising of the sun upon this blight of sand, nor the appearance of a cattle herd, and both black curly and yellow driving it among its dust clouds, warmed my frozen attention as I lay in a sort of spell. I saw with apathy the mountains, extraordinary in the crystal prism of the air, and soon after the strangest scene I have ever looked on by the light of day. For as we went along the driver would give a cry, and when an answering cry came from the thorn-bush we stopped, and a naked Indian would appear,

40

running, to receive a little parcel of salt or sugar or tobacco he had yesterday given the driver some humble coin to buy for him in Thomas. With changeless pagan eyes staring a moment at me on my sack of grain, and a grunt when his purchase was set in his hands, each black-haired desert figure turned away, the bare feet moving silent, and the copper body, stark naked except the breech-clout, receding to dimness in the thorn-bush. But I lay incurious at this new vision of what our wide continent holds in fee under the single title United States, until breakfast came. This helped me, and I livened somewhat at finding the driver and the breakfast man were both genuine Meakums, as Jenks had told me they would be.

It surprised me to discover now that I was looked for along the Gila, and my name approximately known, and when I asked if my friend Captain Stirling had spoken of my coming, it was evidently not he, but the news was in the air. This was a prominence I had never attained in any previous part of the world, and I said to the driver that I supposed my having no business made me a curiosity. That might have something to do with it, he answered (he seemed to have a literal mind), but some had thought I was the paymaster.

"Folks up here," he explained, "are liable to know who's coming."

"If I lived here," said I, "I should be anxious for the paymaster to come early and often."

"Well, it does the country good. The soldiers spend it all right here, and us civilians profit some by it."

Having got him into conversation, I began to introduce the subject of black curly, hoping to lead up to the Widow Sproud; but before I had compassed this we reached San Carlos, where a blow awaited me. Stirling, my host, had been detailed on a scout this morning! I was stranded here, a stranger, where I had come thousands of miles to see an old friend. His regret and messages to make myself at home, and the quartermaster's hearty will to help me to do so could not cure my blankness. He might be absent two weeks or more. I looked round at Carlos and its staring sand. Then I resolved to go at once to my other friends now stationed at Fort Grant. For I had begun to feel myself at an immense distance from any who would care what happened to me for good or ill, and I longed to see some face I had known before. So in gloom I retraced some unattractive steps. This same afternoon I staged back along the sordid, incompetent Gila River, and to kill time pushed my Sproud inquiry, at length with success. To check the inevitably slipshod morals of a frontier commonwealth, Arizona has a statute that in reality only sets in writing a presumption of the common law, the ancient presumption of marriage, which is that when a man and woman go to house-keeping for a certain length of time, they shall be deemed legally married. In Arizona this period is set at twelve months, and ten had run against Mrs. Sproud and young Follet. He was showing signs of leaving her. The driver did not think her much entitled to sympathy, and certainly she showed later that she could devise revenge. As I thought over these things we came again to the cattle herd, where my reappearance astonished yellow and black curly. Nor did the variance between my movements and my reported plans seem wholly explained to them by Stirling's absence, and at the station where I had breakfasted I saw them question the driver about me. This interest in my affairs heightened my desire to reach Fort Grant; and when next day I came to it after another waking to the chanted antiphonals and another faint reveille from Camp Thomas in the waning dark, extreme comfort spread through me. I sat in the club with the officers, and they taught me a new game of cards called Solo, and filled my glass. Here were lieutenants, captains, a major, and a colonel, American citizens with a love of their country and a standard of honor; here floated our bright flag serene against the lofty blue, and the mellow horns sounded at guard-mounting, bringing moisture to the eyes. The day was punctuated with the bright trumpet, people went and came in the simple dignity of duty, and once again I talked with good men and women. God bless our soldier people! I said it often.

CHAPTER V

They somewhat derided my uneasiness in the Gila Valley, and found my surmisings sensational. Yet still they agreed much ready money was an unwise thing on a stage journey, although their profession (I suppose) led them to take being "held up" less seriously than I with my peaceful traditions of elevators and the down-town lunch. In the wide Sulphur Springs valley where I rode at large, but never so long or so far that Fort Grant lay not in sight across that miracle of air, it displeased me to come one morning upon yellow and black curly jogging along beneath the government telegraph line.

"You cover a wide range," said I.

"Cowboys have to," they answered. "So you've not quit us yet?"

"I'm thinking of taking a hunt and fish towards Fort Apache."

"We're your men, then. You'll find us at Thomas any time. We're gathering stock up these draws, but that 'll be through this week."

They spurred their horses and vanished among the steep little hills that run up to Mount Graham. But indeed they should be no men of mine! Stirling had written me his scout was ended, and San Carlos worth a longer visit than I had made there, promising me an escort should I desire to camp in the mountains. An escort it should be, and no yellow or black curly, over-curious about my private matters! This fell in excellently with the coming paymaster's movements. Major Pidcock was even now on his way to Fort Grant from Fort Bowie; and when he went to Thomas and Carlos I would go, too, in his ambulance; and I sighed with pleasure at escaping that stage again.

Major Pidcock arrived in a yellow duster, but in other respects differed from the Bishop, though in his body a bulky man. We were introduced to each other at the club.

"I am glad, sir, to meet you at last," I said to him. "The whole Gila Valley has been taking me for you."

"Oh—ah!" said Pidcock, vaguely, and

pulling at some fat papers in his coat; "indeed. I understand that is a very ignorant population. Colonel Vincent, a word with you. The Department Commander requests me—" And here he went off into some official talk with the Colonel.

I turned among the other officers, who were standing by an open locker having whiskey, and Major Evlie put his hand on my shoulder. "He doesn't mean anything," he whispered, while the rest looked knowingly at me. Presently the Colonel explained to Pidcock that he would have me to keep him company to Carlos.

"Oh—ah, Colonel. Of course we don't take civilians not employed by the government, as a rule. But exceptions—ah—can be made," he said to me. "I will ask you to be ready immediately after breakfast tomorrow." And with that he bowed to us all and sailed forth across the parade-ground.

The Colonel's face was red, and he swore in his quiet voice; but the lips of the lieutenants by the open locker quivered fitfully in the silence.

"Don't mind Pidcock," Evlie remarked. "He's a paymaster." And at this the line officers became disorderly, and two lieutenants danced together; so that, without catching Evlie's evidently military joke, I felt pacified.

"And I've got to have him to dinner,"
sighed the Colonel, and wandered away.

"You'll get on with him, man—you'll get
on with him in the ambulance," said my
friend Paisley. "Flatter him, man. Just ask
him about his great strategic stroke at Cay-
use Station that got him his promotion to
the pay department."

Well, we made our start after breakfast,
Major Pidcock and I, and another passenger too, who sat with the driver—a black
cook going to the commanding officer's at
Thomas. She was an old plantation mammy,
with a kind but bewildered face, and I am
sorry that the noise of our driving lost me
much of her conversation; for whenever we
slowed, and once when I walked up a hill, I
found her remarks to be steeped in a flighty
charm.

"Fo' Lawd's sake!" said she. "W'at's dat?"
And when the driver told her that it was a
jack-rabbit, "You go 'long!" she cried, out-
raged. "I'se seed rabbits earlier 'n de
mawnin' dan yo'self." She watched the animal with all her might, muttering, "Law,
see him squot," and "Hole on, hole on!" and
"Yasser, he done gone fo' sho. My grashus,
you lemme have a scatter shoot-gun an' a
spike-tail smell dog, an' I'll git one of dey
narrah-gauge mules."

"I shall not notice it," said Major Pidcock
to me, with dignity. "But they should have

sent such a creature by the stage. It's unsuitable, wholly."

"Unquestionably," said I, straining to catch the old lady's song on the box:

" 'Don't you fo'git I's a-comin' behind
    you—
    Lam slam de lunch ham.' "

"This is insufferable," said Pidcock. "I shall put her off at Cedar Springs."

I suppose the drive was long to him, but to me it was not. Noon and Cedar Springs prematurely ended the first half of this day most memorable in the whole medley of my excursion, and we got down to dine. Two travellers bound for Thomas by our same road were just setting out, but they firmly declined to transport our cook, and Pidcock moodily saw them depart in their wagon, leaving him burdened still; for this was the day the stage made its down trip from Thomas. Never before had I seen water paid for. When the Major, with windy importance, came to settle his bill, our dozen or fourteen escort horses and mules made an item, the price of watering two head being two bits, quite separate from the feed; and I learned that water was thus precious over most of the Territory.

Our cook remounted the box in high feather, and began at once to comment upon Arizona. "Dere ain't no winter, nor no spring, nor no rain de hole year roun'. My! what a country fo' to gib de chick'ns courage! Dey hens must jus' sit an' lay an' lay. But de po' ducks done have a mean time.

" 'O—Lawd!
  Sinner is in my way, Daniel.' "

"I would not permit a cook like that inside my house," said Major Pidcock.

"She may not be dangerous," I suggested.

"Land! is dey folks gwineter shoot me?" Naturally I looked, and so did the Major; but it was two of our own mounted escort that she saw out to the right of us among the hills. "Tell dem nigger jockeys I got no money. Why do dey triflin' chillun ride in de kerridge?" She did not mean ourselves, but the men with their carbines in the escort wagon in front of us. I looked out at them, and their mouths were wide open for joy at her. It was not a stately progress for twenty-eight thousand dollars in gold and a paymaster to be making. Major Pidcock unbuttoned his duster and reclined to sleep, and presently I also felt the after-dinner sloth shutting my eyes pleasantly to this black road.

"Heave it, chillun! can't you heave?" I heard our cook say, and felt us stop.

"What's that?" I asked, drowsily.

"Seems to be a rock fallen down," the Major answered. "Start it, men; roll it!"

I roused myself. We were between rocks and banks on the brow of a hill, down which the narrow road descended with a slight turn. I could see the escort wagon halted ahead of us, and beyond it the men stooping at a large stone, around which there was no possible room to drive. This stone had fallen, I reflected, since those travellers for Thomas—

There was a shot, and a mule rolled over.

I shall never forget that. It was like the theatre for one paralyzed second! The black soldiers, the mule, the hill, all a clear picture seen through an opera-glass, stock-still, and nothing to do with me—for a congealed second. And, dear me, what a time we had then!

Crackings volleyed around us, puffs of smoke jetted blue from rock ramparts which I had looked at and thought natural—or, rather, not thought of at all—earth and gravel spattered up from the ground, the bawling negress spilled off her box and ran in spirals, screaming, "Oh, bless my soul, bless my soul!" and I saw a yellow duster flap out of the ambulance. "Lawd grashus, he's a-leavin' us!" screeched the cook, and she changed her spirals for a bee-line after him. I should never have run but for this example, for I have not naturally

51

the presence of mind, and in other accidents through which I have passed there has never been promptness about me; the reasoning and all has come when it was over, unless it went on pretty long, when I have been sometimes able to leap to a conclusion. But yes, I ran now, straight under a screen of rocks, over the top of which rose the heads of yellow and black curly. The sight of them sent rushing over me the first agreeable sensation I had felt—shapeless rage—and I found myself shouting at them, "Scoundrels! scoundrels!" while shooting continued briskly around me. I think my performance would have sincerely entertained them could they have spared the time for it; and as it was, they were regarding me with obvious benevolence, when Mr. Adams looked evilly at me across the stones, and black curly seized the old devil's rifle in time to do me a good turn. Mr. Adams's bullet struck short of me ten feet, throwing the earth in my face. Since then I have felt no sympathy for that tobacco-running pioneer. He listened, coughing, to what black curly said as he pointed to me, and I see now that I have never done a wiser thing than to go unarmed in that country. Curly was telling Mr. Adams that I was harmless. Indeed, that was true! In the bottom of this cup, target for a circled rim of rifles, separated from the widely scattered

Major and his men, aware of nothing in particular, and seeing nothing in particular but smoke and rocks and faces peering everywhere, I walked to a stone and sat upon it, hypnotized again into a spectator. From this undisturbed vantage I saw shape itself the theft of the gold—the first theft, that is; for it befell me later to witness a ceremony by which these eagles of Uncle Sam again changed hands in a manner that stealing is as good a name for as any.

They had got two mules killed, so that there could be no driving away in a hurry, and I saw that killing men was not a part of their war, unless required as a means to their end. Major Pidcock had spared them this necessity; I could see him nowhere; and with him to imitate I need not pause to account for the members of our dismounted escort. Two soldiers, indeed, lay on the ground, the sergeant and another, who had evidently fired a few resisting shots; but let me say at once that these poor fellows recovered, and I saw them often again through this adventure that bound us together, else I could not find so much hilarity in my retrospect. Escort wagon and ambulance stood empty and foolish on the road, and there lay the ingenious stone all by itself, and the carbines all by themselves foolish in the wagon, where the innocent soldiers had left them on getting out to move the stone. Smoke loitered thin and blue over this now exceedingly quiet scene, and I smelt it where I sat. How secure the robbers had felt themselves, and how reckless of identification! Mid-day, a public road within hearing of a ranch, an escort of a dozen regulars, no masks, and the stroke perpetrated at the top of a descent, contrary to all laws of road agency. They swarmed into sight from their ramparts. I cannot tell what number, but several I had never seen before and never saw again; and Mr. Adams and yellow and black curly looked so natural that I wondered if Jenks and the Bishop would come climbing down too. But no more old friends turned up that day. Some went to the ambulance swift and silent, while others most needlessly stood guard. Nothing was in sight but my seated inoffensive form, and the only sound was, somewhere among the rocks, the voice of the incessant negress speeding through her prayers. I saw them at the ambulance, surrounding, passing, lifting, stepping in and out, ferreting, then moving slowly up with their booty round the hill's brow. Then silence; then hoofs; then silence again, except the outpouring negress, scriptural, melodious, symbolic:

    " 'Oh—Lawd!
      Sinner is in my way, Daniel.' "

All this while I sat on the stone. "They have done us brown," I said aloud, and hearing my voice waked me from whatever state I had been in. My senses bounded, and I ran to the hurt soldiers. One was very sick. I should not have known what to do for them, but people began to arrive, brought from several quarters by the fusillade—two in a wagon from Cedar Springs, two or three on horses from the herds they were with in the hills, and a very old man from somewhere, who offered no assistance to any one, but immediately seated himself and began explaining what we all should have done. The negress came out of her rocks, exclamatory with pity over the wounded, and, I am bound to say, of more help to them than any of us, kind and motherly in the midst of her ceaseless discourse. Next arrived Major Pidcock in his duster, and took charge of everything.

"Let yer men quit the'r guns, did ye, general?" piped the very old man. "Escort oughtn't never to quit the'r guns. I seen that at Molino del Rey. And ye should have knowed that there stone didn't crawl out in the road like a turtus to git the sunshine."

"Where were you?" thundered the Major to the mounted escort, who now appeared, half an hour after the event, from our flanks, which they had been protecting at an immense distance. "Don't you know your duty's to be on hand when you hear firing?"

"Law, honey!" said the cook, with a guffaw, "lemme git my han's over my mouf."

"See them walls they fooled yer with!" continued the old man, pointing with his stick. "I could have told yer them wasn't natural. Them doesn't show like country rock;" by which I found that he meant their faces were new-exposed and not weather-beaten.

"No doubt you could have saved us, my friend," said the Major, puffing blandly.

But one cannot readily impress ninety summers. "Yes, I could have told yer that," assented the sage, with senile complacence. "My wife could have told yer that. Any smart girl could have told yer that."

"I shall send a despatch for re-enforcements," annnounced Pidcock. "Tap the telegraph wire," he ordered.

"I have to repawt to the Major," said a soldier, saluting, "dat de line is cut."

At this I was taken with indecent laughter, and turned away, while ninety summers observed, "Of course them boys would cut the wire if they knew their business."

Swearing capably, the Major now accounted clearly to us for the whole occurrence, striding up and down, while we lifted the hurt men into the ranch wagon, and arranged for their care at Cedar Springs. The escort wagon hurried on to Thomas for a doctor. The ambulance was, of course, crippled of half its team, and the dead mules were cleared from their harness and got to the road-side. Having satisfactorily delivered himself of his explanation, the Major now organized a party for following the trail of the robbers, to learn into what region they had betaken themselves. Incredible as it may seem, after my late unenterprising conduct, I asked one of the riders to lend me his horse, which he did, remarking that he should not need it for an hour, and that he was willing to risk my staying absent longer than that.

So we rode away. The trail was clear, and we had but little trouble to follow it. It took us off to the right through a mounded labyrinth of hillocks, puny and gray like ash-heaps, where we rose and fell in the trough of the sullen landscape. I told Pidcock of my certainty about three of the robbers, but he seemed to care nothing for this, and was something less than civil at what he called my suggestions.

"When I have ascertained their route," he said, "it will be time enough to talk of their identity."

In this way we went for a mile or so, the trail leading us onward, frank and straight, to the top of a somewhat higher hill, where it suddenly expired off the earth. No breath vanishes cleaner from glass, and it brought us to a dead halt. We retraced the tracks to make sure we had not lost them before, but there was no mistake, and again we halted dead at the vanishing-point. Here were signs that something out of the common had happened. Men's feet and horseshoe prints, aimless and superimposed, marked a trodden frame of ground, inside which was nothing, and beyond which nothing lay but those faint tracks of wandering cattle and horses that scatter everywhere in this country. Not one defined series, not even a single shod horse, had gone over this hill, and we spent some minutes vainly scouring in circles wider and wider. Often I returned to stare at the trodden, imperturbable frame of ground, and caught myself inspecting first the upper air, and next the earth, and speculating if the hill were hollow; and mystery began to film over the hitherto sharp figures of black curly and yellow, while the lonely country around grew so unpleasant to my nerves that I was glad when Pidcock decided that he must give up for to-day. We found the little group of people beginning to disperse at the ambulance.

"Fooled yer ag'in, did they?" said the old man. "Played the blanket trick on yer, I expect. Guess yer gold's got pretty far by now." With this parting, and propped upon his stick, he went as he had come. Not even at any time of his youth, I think, could he have been companionable, and old age had certainly filled him with the impartial malevolence of the devil. I rejoice to say that he presided at none of our further misadventures.

CHAPTER VI

Short twenty-eight thousand dollars and two mules, we set out anew, the Major, the cook, and I, along the Thomas road, with the sun drawing closer down upon the long steel saw that the peaks to our westward made. The site of my shock lay behind me—I knew now well enough that it had been a shock, and that for a long while to come I should be able to feel the earth spatter from Mr. Adams's bullet against my ear and sleeve whenever I might choose to conjure that moment up again—and the present comfort in feeling my distance from that stone in the road increase continually put me in more cheerful spirits. With the quick rolling of the wheels many subjects

61

for talk came into my mind, and had I been seated on the box beside the cook we should have found much in common. Ever since her real tenderness to those wounded men I had wished to ask the poor old creature how she came in this weary country, so far from the pleasant fields of cotton and home. Her hair was gray, and she had seen much, else she had never been so kind and skilful at bandaging. And I am quite sure that somewhere in the chambers of her incoherent mind and simple heart abided the sweet ancient fear of God and love of her fellow-men—virtues I had met but little in Arizona.

"De hole family, scusin' two," she was saying, "dey bust loose and tuck to de woods." And then she moralized upon the two who stayed behind and were shot. "But de Gennul he 'low dat wuz mighty pore reasonin'."

I should have been glad to exchange views with her, for Major Pidcock was dull company. This prudent officer was not growing distant from his disaster, and as night began to come, and we neared Thomas, I suppose the thought that our ambulance was driving him perhaps to a court-martial was enough to submerge the man in gloom. To me and my news about the robbers he was a little more considerate, although he still made nothing of the fact that some of them lived in the Gila Valley, and were of the patriarchal tribe of Meakum.

"Scoundrels like that," he muttered, lugubriously, "know every trail in the country, and belong nowhere. Mexico is not a long ride from here. They can get a steamer at Guaymas and take their choice of ports down to Valparaiso. Yes, they'll probably spend that money in South America. Oh, confound that woman!"

For the now entirely cheerful negress was singing:

" 'Dar's de gal, dar's my Susanna.
    How by gum you know?
    Know her by de red bandanna,
    An' de shoestring hangin' on de flo'—
    Dad blam her!—
    An' de shoestring hangin'—

Goodness grashus! what *you* gwineter do?"

At this sudden cry and the stopping of the ambulance I thought more people were come for our gold, and my spirit resigned itself. Sit still was all I should do now, and look for the bright day when I should leave Arizona forever. But it was only Mrs. Sproud. I had clean forgotten her, and did not at once take in to what an important turn the affairs of some of us had come. She stepped out of the darkness, and put her hand on the door of the ambulance.

"I suppose you're the Paymaster?" Her voice was soft and easy, but had an ample volume. As Pidcock was replying with some dignity that she was correct, she caught sight of me. "Who is this man?" she interrupted him.

"My clerk," said Pidcock; and this is the promptest thing I can remember of the Major, always excepting his conduct when the firing began on the hill. "You're asking a good many questions, madam," he added.

"I want to know who I'm talking to," said she, quietly. "I think I've seen property of yours this evening."

"You had better get in, madam; better get in."

"This is the Paymaster's team from Fort Grant?" said Mrs. Sproud to the driver.

"Yes, yes, madam. Major Pidcock—I am Major Pidcock, Paymaster to the United States army in the Department of Colorado. I suppose I understand you."

"Seven canvas sacks," said Mrs. Sproud, standing in the road.

"Get in, madam. You can't tell who may be within hearing. You will find it to your advantage to keep nothing—"

Mrs. Sproud laughed luxuriously, and I began to discern why black curly might at times have been loath to face her.

"I merely meant, madam—I desired to make it clear that—a—"

"I think I know what you meant. But I have no call to fear the law. It will save you trouble to believe that before we go any further."

"Certainly, madam. Quite right." The man was sweating. What with court-martial and Mrs. Sproud, his withers were wrung. "You are entirely sure, of course, madam—"

"I am entirely sure I know what I am about. That seems to be more than some do that are interested in this gold—the folks, for instance, that have hid it in my hay-stack."

"Hay-stack! Then they're not gone to Mexico!"

"Mexico, sir? They live right here in this valley. Now I'll get in, and when I ask you, you will please to set me down." She seated herself opposite us and struck a match. "Now we know what we all look like," said she, holding the light up, massive and handsome. "This young man is the clerk, and we needn't mind him. I have done nothing to fear the law, but what I am doing now will make me a traveller again. I have no friends here. I was acquainted with a young man." She spoke in the serenest tone, but let fall the match more quickly than its burning made needful. "He was welcome in my home. He let them cook this up in my house and never told me. I live a good ways out

65

on the road, and it was a safe place, but I didn't think why so many met him, and why they sat around my stable. Once in a while this week they've been joking about winning the soldiers' pay—they often win that—but I thought it was just cowboy games, till I heard horses coming quick at sundown this afternoon, and I hid. Will hunted around and said—and said I was on the stage coming from Solomonsville, and so they had half an hour yet. He thought so. And, you see, nobody lives in the cabin but—but me." Mrs. Sproud paused a moment here, and I noticed her breathing. Then she resumed: "So I heard them talk some; and when they all left, pretty soon, I went to the hay-stack, and it was so. Then the stage came along and I rode to Thomas."

"You left the gold there!" groaned the wretched Major, and leaned out of the ambulance.

"I'm not caring to touch what's none of mine. Wait, sir, please; I get out here. Here are the names I'm sure of. Stop the driver, or I'll jump." She put a paper in the Major's hand. "It is Mrs. Sproud's hay-stack," she added.

"Will you—this will never—can I find you to-morrow?" he said, helplessly, holding the paper out at her.

66

"I have told you all I know," said Mrs. Sproud, and was gone at once.

Major Pidcock leaned back for some moments as we drove. Then he began folding his paper with care. "I have not done with that person," said he, attempting to restore his crippled importance. "She will find that she must explain herself."

Our wheels whirled in the sand and we came quickly to Thomas, to a crowd of waiting officers and ladies; and each of us had an audience that night—the cook, I feel sure, while I myself was of an importance second only to the Major's. But he was at once closeted with the commanding officer, and I did not learn their counsels, hearing only at breakfast that the first step was taken. The detail sent out had returned from the hay-stack, bringing gold indeed— one-half sackful. The other six were gone, and so was Mrs. Sproud. It was useless to surmise, as we, however, did that whole forenoon, what any of this might mean; but in the afternoon came a sign. A citizen of the Gila Valley had been paying his many debts at the saloon and through the neighborhood in gold. In one well known for the past two years to be without a penny it was the wrong moment to choose for honest affluence, and this citizen was the first arrest. This further instance of how secure the robbers felt themselves to be outdid anything that had happened yet, and I marvelled until following events took from me the power of astonishment. The men named on Mrs. Sproud's paper were fewer than I think fired upon us in the attack, but every one of them was here in the valley, going about his business. Most were with the same herd of cattle that I had seen driven by yellow and black curly near the sub-agency, and they two were there. The solvent debtor, I should say, was not arrested this morning. Plans that I, of course, had no part in delayed matters, I suppose for the sake of certainty. Black curly and his friends were watched, and found to be spending no gold yet; and since they did not show sign of leaving the region, but continued with their cattle, I imagine every effort was being made to light upon their hidden treasure. But their time came, and soon after it mine. Stirling, my friend, to whom I had finally gone at Carlos, opened the wire door of his quarters where I sat one morning, and with a heartless smile introduced me to a gentleman from Tucson.

"You'll have a chance to serve your country," said Stirling.

I was subpoenaed!

"Certainly not!" I said, with indignation. "I'm going East. I don't live here. You have witnesses enough without me. We all saw the same thing."

"Witnesses never see the same thing," observed the man from Tucson. "It's the government that's after you. But you'll not have to wait. Our case is first on the list."

"You can take my deposition," I began; but what need to dwell upon this interview? "When I come to visit you again," I said to Stirling, "let me know." And that pink-faced, gray-haired captain still shouted heartlessly.

"You're an egotist," said he. "Think of the scrape poor old Pidcock has got himself into."

"The government needs all the witnesses it can get," said the man from Tucson. "Luke Jenks is smart in some ways."

"Luke Jenks?" I sat up in my canvas extension-chair.

"Territorial Delegate; firm of Parley and Jenks, Tucson. He's in it."

"By heavens!" I cried, in unmixed delight. "But I didn't see him when they were shooting at us."

The man from Tucson stared at me curiously. "He is counsel for the prisoners," he explained.

"The Delegate to Washington defends these thieves who robbed the United States?" I repeated.

"Says he'll get them off. He's going to stay home from Washington and put it through in shape."

It was here that my powers of astonishment went into their last decline, and I withheld my opinion upon the character of Mr. Jenks as a public man. I settled comfortably in my canvas chair.

"The prisoners are citizens of small means, I judge," said I. "What fee can they pay for such a service?"

"Ah!" said Stirling.

"That's about it, I guess," said the man from Tucson. "Luke is mighty smart in his law business. Well, gents, good-day to you. I must be getting after the rest of my witnesses."

"Have you seen Mrs. Sproud?" I asked him.

"She's quit the country. We can't trace her. Guess she was scared."

"But that gold!" I exclaimed, when Stirling and I were alone. "What in the world have they done with those six other bags?"

"Ah!" said he, as before. "Do you want to bet on that point? Dollars to doughnuts Uncle Sam never sees a cent of that money again. I'll stake my next quarter's pay—"

"Pooh!" said I. "That's poor odds against doughnuts if Pidcock has the paying of it." And I took my turn at laughing at the humorous Stirling.

"That Mrs. Sproud is a sensible woman to have gone," said he, reflectively. "They would know she had betrayed them, and she wouldn't be safe in the valley. Witnesses who know too much sometimes are found dead in this country—but you'll have government protection."

"Thank you kindly," said I. "That's what I had on the hill."

But Stirling took his turn at me again with freshened mirth.

CHAPTER VII

Well, I think that we witnesses were worth government protection. At seasons of especial brightness and holiday, such as Christmas and Easter, the theatres of the variety order have a phrase which they sometimes print in capitals upon their bills—Combination Extraordinary; and when you consider Major Pidcock and his pride, and the old plantation cook, and my reserved Eastern self, and our coal-black escort of the hill, more than a dozen, including Sergeant Brown and the private, both now happily recovered of their wounds, you can see what appearance we made descending together from the mean Southern Pacific train at Tucson, under the gaze of what I take to have been the town's whole population, numbering five thousand.

Stirling, who had come to see us through, began at his persiflage immediately, and congratulated me upon the house I should play to, speaking of box-office receipts and a benefit night. Tucson is more than half a Mexican town, and in its crowd upon the platform I saw the gaudy shawls, the ear-rings, the steeple straw hats, the old shrivelled cigarette-rolling apes, and the dark-eyed girls, and sifted with these the loungers of our own race, boots, overalls, pistols, hotel clerks, express agents, freight hands, waitresses, red-shirts, soldiers from Lowell Barracks, and officers, and in this mass and mess of color and dust and staring, Bishop Meakum in his yellow duster, by the door of the Hotel San Xavier. But his stare was not, I think now, quite of the same idleness with the rest. He gave me a short nod, yet not unfriendly, as I passed by him to register my name. By the counter I found the wet-eyed Mowry standing.

"How's business on the other side of the track?" I said to him.

"Fair to middlin'. Get them mines ye was after at Globe?"

"You've forgotten I told you they're a property I don't care for, Mr. Mowry. I suppose it's interest in this recent gold discovery that brings you to Tucson." He had no answer for me but a shrewd shirking glance that flattered my sense of acumen, and adding, pleasantly, "So many of your Arizona citizens have forsaken silver for gold just now," I wrote my name in the hotel book, while he looked to remind himself what it was.

"Why, you're not to stay here," said Stirling, coming up. "You're expected at the Barracks."

He presented me at once to a knot of officers, each of whom in turn made me known to some additional by-stander, until it seemed to me that I shook a new hand sixty times in this disordered minute by the hotel book, and out of the sixty caught one name, which was my own.

These many meetings could not be made perfect without help from the saloon-keeper, who ran his thriving trade conveniently at hand in the office of the San Xavier. Our group remained near him, and I silently resolved to sleep here at the hotel, away from the tempting confusion of army hospitality upon this eve of our trial. We were expected, however, to dine at the post, and that I was ready to do. Indeed, I could scarcely have got myself out of it without rudeness, for the ambulance was waiting us guests at the gate. We went to it along a latticed passage at the edge of a tropical garden, only a few square yards in all, but how pretty! and what an oasis of calm in the midst of this teeming desolation of unrest! It had upon one side the railway station, wooden, sordid, congesting with malodorous packed humanity; on the next the rails themselves and the platform, with steam and bells and baggage trucks rolling and bumping; the hotel stood on the third, a confusion of tongues and trampings; while a wide space of dust, knee-deep, and littered with manoeuvring vehicles, hemmed in this silent garden on the fourth side. A slender slow little fountain dropped inaudibly among some palms, a giant cactus, and the broad-spread shade of trees I did not know. This was the whole garden, and a tame young antelope was its inhabitant. He lay in the unchanging shade, his large eyes fixed remotely upon the turmoil of this world, and a sleepy charm touched my senses as I looked at his domain. Instead of going to dinner, or going anywhere, I should have liked to recline indefinitely beneath those palms and trail my fingers in the cool fountain. Such enlightened languor, however, could by no happy chance be the lot of an important witness in a Western robbery trial, and I dined and wined with the jovial officers, at least talking no business.

With business I was sated. Pidcock and the attorney for the United States—I can remember neither his name nor the proper title of his office, for he was a nobody, and I had forgotten his features each new time that we met—had mapped out the trial to me, preparing and rehearsing me in my testimony until they had pestered me into a hatred of them both. And when word was brought me here, dining at Lowell Barracks, where I had imagined myself safe from justice, that this same attorney was waiting to see me, I rose and I played him a trick. Possibly I should not have done it but for the saloon-keeper in the afternoon and this sustained dining now; but I sent him word I should be with him directly— and I wandered into Tucson by myself!

Faithful to my last strong impression there, I went straight to the tiny hotel garden, and in that darkness lay down in a delicious and torpid triumph. The attorney was most likely waiting still. No one on earth knew where I was. Pidcock could not trace me now. I could see the stars through the palms and the strange trees, the fountain made a little sound, somewhere now and then I could hear the antelope, and, cloaked in this black serenity, I lay smiling. Once an engine passed heavily, leaving the station utterly quiet again, and the next I knew it was the antelope's rough tongue that waked me, and I found him nibbling and licking my hand. People were sitting in the latticed passage, and from the light in the office came Mr. Mowry, untying a canvas sack that he held. At this sight my truancy to discretion was over, and no head could be more wakeful or clear than mine instantly became.

"How much d'yer want this time, Mr. Jenks?" inquired Mowry.

I could not hear the statesman's reply, but thought, while the sound of clinking came to me, how a common cause will often serve to reconcile the most bitter opponents. I did not dare go nearer to catch all their talk, and I debated a little upon my security even as it was, until my own name suddenly reached me.

"Him?" said Mowry; "that there tailor-made boy? They've got him sleepin' at the Barracks."

"Nobody but our crowd's boarding here," said some one.

"They think we're laying for their witnesses," said the voice of Jenks. And among the various mingled laughs rose distinct a big one that I knew.

"Oh, ho, ho! Well, yes. Tell you about witnesses. Here's all there is to them: spot cash to their figure, and kissing the Book. You've done no work but what I told you?" he added, sharply.

"We haven't needed to worry about witnesses in any shape, Bishop."

"That's good. That's economy. That little Eastern toorist is harmless."

"Leave him talk, Bishop. Leave 'em all tell their story."

"It's going to cost the whole stake, though," said Jenks.

"Deserted Jericho!" remarked old Meakum.

"I don't try cases for nothing, Bishop. The deal's covered. My clients have publicly made over to me their horses and saddles."

"Oh, ho, ho!" went the Bishop. But this last word about the horses was the only part of the talk I could not put a plain meaning upon.

Mr. Mowry I now saw re-enter the lighted door of the office, with his canvas sack in his hand. "This 'll be right here in the safe," said he.

"All right," answered Jenks. "I'll not be likely to call on you any more for a day or so."

"Hello!" said the office clerk, appearing in his shirtsleeves. "You fellows have made me forget the antelope." He took down a lantern, and I rose to my feet.

"Give us a drink before you feed him," said Jenks. Then I saw the whole of them crowd into the door for their nightcap, and that was all I waited for.

I climbed the garden fence. My thoughts led me at random through quantities of soft dust, and over the rails, I think, several times, until I stood between empty and silent freight trains, and there sat down. Harmless! It seemed to me they would rate me differently in the morning. So for a while my mind was adrift in the turbulent cross-currents of my discovery; but it was with a smooth, innocent surface that I entered the hotel office and enjoyed the look of the clerk when he roused and heard me, who, according to their calculations, should have been in slumber at the Barracks, asking to be shown my room here. I was tempted to inquire if he had fed the antelope—such was the pride of my elation—and I think he must have been running over questions to put me; but the two of us marched up the stairs with a lamp and a key, speaking amiably of the weather for this time of year, and he unlocked my door with a politeness and hoped I would sleep well with a consideration that I have rarely met in the hotel clerk. I did not sleep well. Yet it seemed not to matter. By eight I had breakfast, and found the attorney—Rocklin I shall name him, and that will have to answer—and told him how we had become masters of the situation.

He made me repeat it all over, jotting memoranda this second time; and when my story was done, he sat frowning at his notes, with a cigar between his teeth.

"This ain't much," he said. "Luckily I don't need anything more. I've got a dead open-and-shut case without it."

"Why don't you make it deader, then?" said I. "Don't you see what it all means?"

"Well, what does it all mean?"

Either the man was still nettled at my treatment of him last evening, or had no liking for amateur opinions and help; otherwise I see no reason for the disparagement with which he regarded me while I interpreted what I had overheard, piece by piece, except the horse and saddle remark.

"Since that don't seem clear, I'll explain it to you," he said, "and then you'll know it all. Except their horses and saddles, the accused haven't a red cent to their names—not an honest one, that is. So it looks well for them to be spending all they've apparently got in the world to pay counsel fees. Now I have this case worked up," he pursued, complacently, "so that any such ambiguous stuff as yours is no good to me at all—would be harmful, in fact. It's not good policy, my friend, to assail the character of opposing counsel. And Bishop Meakum! Are you aware of his power and standing in this section? Do you think you're going to ring him in?"

"Great goodness!" I cried. "Let me testify, and then let the safe be opened."

Rocklin looked at me a moment, the cigar

wagging between his teeth, and then he lightly tossed his notes in the waste-paper basket.

"Open your safe," said he, "and what then? Up steps old Mowry and says, 'I'll thank you to let my property alone.' Where's your proof? What word did any of them drop that won't bear other constructions? Mowry's well known to have money, and he has a right to give it to Jenks."

"If the gold could be identified?" I suggested.

"That's been all attended to," he answered, with increasing complacence. "I'm obliged to you for your information, and in a less sure case I might risk using it, but— why, see here; we've got 'em hands down!" And he clapped me on the knee. "If I had met you last evening I was going to tell you our campaign. Pidcock 'll come first, of course, and his testimony 'll cover pretty much the whole ground. Then, you see, the rest of you I'll use mainly in support. Sergeant Brown—he's very strong, and the black woman, and you—I'll probably call you third or fourth. So you'll be on hand sure now?"

Certainly I had no thought of being anywhere else. The imminence of our trial was now heralded by the cook's coming to Rocklin's office punctual to his direction, and after her Pidcock almost immediately. It was not many minutes before the more important ones of us had gathered, and we proceeded to court, once again a Combination Extraordinary—a spectacle for Tucson. So much stir and prosperity had not blossomed in the town for many years, its chief source of life being the money that Lowell Barracks brought to it. But now its lodgings were crowded and its saloons and Mexican dens of entertainment waked to activity. From a dozing sunburnt village of adobe walls and almond-trees it was become something like those places built in a single Western day of riot extravagance, where corner lots are clamored for and men pay a dollar to be shaved.

Jenks was before us in the room with his clients. He was practising what I always think of as his celluloid smile, whispering, and all-hail with everybody. One of the prisoners had just such another mustache as his own, too large for his face; and this had led me since to notice a type of too large mustaches through our country in all ranks, but of similar men, who generally have either stolen something or lacked the opportunity. Catching sight of me, Jenks came at once, friendly as you please, shaking my passive hand, and laughing that we should meet again under such circumstances.

"When we're through this nuisance," said he, "you must take dinner with me. Just now, you understand, it wouldn't look well to see me hobnobbing with a government witness. See you again!" And he was off to some one else.

I am confident this man could not see himself as others—some others, at least—saw him. To him his whole performance was natural and professional, and my view that he was more infamous by far than the thieves would have sincerely amazed him. Indeed, for one prisoner I felt very sorry. Young black curly was sitting there, and, in contrast to Mr. Adams, down whose beard the tobacco forever ran, he seemed downcast and unhardened, I thought. He was getting his deserts through base means. It was not for the sake of justice but from private revenge that Mrs. Sproud had moved; and, after all, had the boy injured her so much as this? Yet how could I help him? They were his deserts. My mood was abruptly changed to diversion when I saw among our jury specimens of both types of Meakum, and prominent among the spectator throng their sire, that canny polygamist, surveying the case with the same forceful attention I had noticed first in the House of Representatives, and ever since that day. But I had a true shock of surprise now. Mrs. Sproud was in court. There could be no mistake. No one seemed to notice her, and I wondered if many in the town knew her face, and with what intent she had returned to this dangerous neighborhood. I was so taken up with watching her and her furtive appearance in the almost concealed position she had chosen that I paid little heed to the government's opening of its case. She had her eyes upon black curly, but he could not see her. Pidcock was in the midst of his pompous recital when the court took its noon intermission. Then I was drawn to seek out black curly as he was conducted to his dinner.

"Good-day," said he, as I came beside him.

"I wish I didn't have to go on oath about this," I said.

"Oath away," he answered, doggedly. "What's that got to do with me?"

"Oh, come!" I exclaimed.

"Come where?" He looked at me defiantly.

"When people don't wish to be trailed," I went on, "do I understand they sometimes spread a blanket and lead their horses on it and take off their shoes? I'm merely asking out of a traveller's curiosity."

"I guess you'll have to ask them that's up on such tricks," he answered, grinning.

I met him in the eyes, and a strong liking for him came over me. "I probably owe you my life," I said, huskily. "I know I do. And

I hate—you must consider me a poor sort of bird."

"Blamed if I know what you're drivin' at," said black curly. But he wrinkled his forehead in the pleasant way I remembered. "Yer whiskey was good all right," he added, and gave me his hand.

"Look here," said I. "She's come back."

This took the boy unguarded, and he swore with surprise. Then his face grew sombre. "Let her," he remarked; and that was all we said.

At the afternoon sitting I began to notice how popular sympathy was not only quite against the United States, but a sentiment amounting to hatred was shown against all soldiers. The voice of respectability seemed entirely silent; decent citizens were there, but not enough of them. The mildest opinion was that Uncle Sam could afford to lose money better than poor people, and the strongest was that it was a pity the soldiers had not been killed. This seemed inappropriate in a Territory desiring admission to our Union. I supposed it something local then, but have since observed it to be a prevailing Western antipathy. The unthinking sons of the sage-brush ill tolerate a thing which stands for discipline, good order, and obedience, and the man who lets another command him they despise. I can think of no threat more evil for our democracy, for it is a fine thing diseased and perverted—namely, independence gone drunk.

Pidcock's examination went forward, and the half-sack of gold from the hay-stack brought a great silence in court. The Major's identification of the gold was conducted by Rocklin with stage effect, for it was an undoubted climax; but I caught a most singular smile on the face of Bishop Meakum, and there sat Mrs. Sproud, still solitary and engulfed in the throng, her face flushed and her eyes blazing. And here ended the first day.

CHAPTER VIII

In the morning came the Major's cross-examination, with the room more crowded than before, but I could not find Mrs. Sproud. Rocklin did not believe I had seen her, and I feared something had happened to her. The Bishop had walked to the court with Jenks, talking and laughing upon general subjects, so far as I could hear. The counsel for the prisoners passed lightly over the first part of the evidence, only causing an occasional laugh on the score of the Major's military prowess, until he came to the gold.

"You said this sack was one of yours, Major?" he now inquired.

"It is mine, sir."

A large bundle of sacks was brought. "And how about these? Here are ten, fifteen—about forty. I'll get some more if you say so. Are they all yours?"

"Your question strikes me as idle, sir." The court rapped, and Jenks smiled. "They resemble mine," said Pidcock. "But they are not used."

"No; not used." Jenks held up the original, shaking the gold. "Now I'm going to empty your sack for a moment."

"I object," said Rocklin, springing up.

"Oh, it's all counted," laughed Jenks; and the objection was not sustained. Then Jenks poured the gold into a new sack and shook that aloft. "It makes them look confusingly similar, Major. I'll just put my card in your sack."

"I object," said Rocklin, with anger, but with futility. Jenks now poured the gold back into the first, then into a third, and thus into several, tossing them each time on the table, and the clinking pieces sounded clear in the room. Bishop Meakum was watching the operation like a wolf. "Now, Major," said Jenks, "is your gold in the original sack, or which sack is my card in?"

This was the first time that the room broke out loudly; and Pidcock, when the people were rapped to order, said, "The sack's not the thing."

"Of course not. The gold is our point. And of course you had a private mark on it. Tell the jury, please, what the private mark was."

He had none. He spoke about dates, and new coins, he backed and filled, swelled importantly, and ended like a pricked bladder by recanting his identification.

"That is all I have to say for the present," said Jenks.

"Don't complicate the issue by attempting to prove too much, Mr. Rocklin," said the judge.

Rocklin flushed, and called the next witness, whispering sulkily to me, "What can you expect if the court starts out against you?" But the court was by no means against him. The judge was merely disgusted over Rocklin's cardinal folly of identifying coin under such loose conditions.

And now came the testimony of Sergeant Brown. He told so clear a story as to chill the enthusiasm of the room. He pointed to the man with the mustache, black curly, and yellow. "I saw them shooting from the right of the road," he said. Jenks tried but little to shake him, and left him unshaken. He was followed by the other wounded soldier, whose story was nearly the same, except that he identified different prisoners.

"Who did you say shot you?" inquired Jenks. "Which of these two?"

"I didn't say. I don't know."

"Don't know a man when he shoots you in broad daylight?"

"Plenty was shooting at me," said the soldier. And his testimony also remained unshaken.

Then came my own examination, and Jenks did not trouble me at all, but, when I had likewise identified the men I knew, simply bowed smilingly, and had no questions to ask his friend from the East.

Our third morning began with the negress, who said she was married, told a scattered tale, and soon stated that she was single, explaining later that she had two husbands, and one was dead, while the other had disappeared from her ten years ago. Gradually her alarm subsided and she achieved coherence.

"What did this gentleman do at the occurrence?" inquired Jenks, indicating me.

"Dat gemman? He jes flew, sir, an' I don' blame him fo' bein' no wusser skeer'd dan de hole party. Yesser, we all flew scusin' dey two pore chillun; an' we stayed till de 'currence was ceased."

"But the gentleman says he sat on a stone, and saw those men firing."

"Land! I seed him goin' like he was gwineter Fo't Grant. He run up de hill, an' de Gennul he run down like de day of judgment."

"The General ran?"

"Lawd grashus, honey, yo' could have played checkers on dey coat tails of his."

The court rapped gently.

"But the gold must have been heavy to carry away to the horses. Did not the General exert his influence to rally his men?"

"No, sah. De Gennul went down de hill, an' he took his inflooence with him."

"I have no further questions," said Jenks. "When we come to our alibis, gentlemen, I expect to satisfy you that this lady saw more correctly, and when she is unable to recognize my clients it is for a good reason."

"We've not got quite so far yet," Rocklin observed. "We've reached the hay-stack at present."

"Aren't you going to make her describe her own confusion more?" I began, but stopped, for I saw that the next witness was at hand, and that it was Mrs. Sproud.

"How's this?" I whispered to Rocklin. "How did you get her?"

"She volunteered this morning, just before trial. We're in big luck."

The woman was simply dressed in something dark. Her handsome face was pale, but she held a steady eye upon the jury, speaking clearly and with deliberation. Old Meakum, always in court and watchful, was plainly unprepared for this, and among the prisoners, too, I could discern uneasiness. Whether or no any threat or constraint had kept her invisible during these days, her coming now was a thing for which none of us were ready.

"What do I know?" she repeated after the counsel. "I suppose you have been told what I said I knew."

"We'd like to hear it directly from you, Mrs. Sproud," Rocklin explained.

"Where shall I start?"

"Well, there was a young man who boarded with you, was there not?"

"I object to the witness being led," said Jenks. And Bishop Meakum moved up beside the prisoners' counsel and began talking with him earnestly.

"Nobody is leading me," said Mrs. Sproud, imperiously, and raising her voice a little. She looked about her. "There was a young man who boarded with me. Of course that is so."

Meakum broke off in his confidences with Jenks, and looked sharply at her.

"Do you see your boarder anywhere here?" inquired Rocklin; and from his tone I perceived that he was puzzled by the manner of his witness.

She turned slowly, and slowly scrutinized the prisoners one by one. The head of black curly was bent down, and I saw her eyes rest upon it while she stood in silence. It was as if he felt the summons of her glance, for he raised his head. His face was scarlet, but her paleness did not change.

"He is the one sitting at the end," she said, looking back at the jury. She then told some useless particulars, and brought her narrative to the afternoon when she had heard the galloping. "Then I hid. I hid because this is a rough country."

"When did you recognize that young man's voice?"

"I did not recognize it."

Black curly's feet scraped as he shifted his position.

"Collect yourself, Mrs. Sproud. We'll give you all the time you want. We know ladies are not used to talking in court. Did you not hear this young man talking to his friends?"

"I heard talking," replied the witness, quite collected. "But I could not make out who they were. If I could have been sure it was him and friends, I wouldn't have stayed hid. I'd have had no call to be scared."

Rocklin was dazed, and his next question came in a voice still more changed and irritable.

"Did you see any one?"

"No one."

"What did you hear them say?"

"They were all talking at once. I couldn't be sure."

"Why did you go to the hay-stack?"

"Because they said something about my hay-stack, and I wanted to find out, if I could."

"Did you not write their names on a paper and give it to this gentleman? Remember you are on oath, Mrs. Sproud."

By this time a smile was playing on the features of Jenks, and he and Bishop Meakum talked no longer together, but sat back to watch the woman's extraordinary attempt to undo her work. It was shrewd, very shrewd, in her to volunteer as our witness instead of as theirs. She was ready for the paper question, evidently.

"I wrote—" she began, but Rocklin interrupted.

"On oath, remember!" he repeated, finding himself cross-examining his own witness. "The names you wrote are the names of these prisoners here before the court. They were traced as the direct result of your information. They have been identified by three or four persons. Do you mean to say you did not know who they were?"

"I did not know," said Mrs. Sproud, firmly. "As for the paper, I acted hasty. I was a woman, alone, and none to consult or advise me. I thought I would get in trouble if I did not tell about such goings on, and I just wrote the names of Will—of the boys that came round there all the time, thinking it was most likely them. I didn't see him, and I didn't make out surely it was his voice. I wasn't sure enough to come out and ask what they were up to. I didn't stop to think of the harm I was doing on guess-work."

For the first time the note of remorse conquered in her voice. I saw how desperation at what she had done when she thought her love was cured was now bracing the woman to this audacity.

"Remember," said Rocklin, "the gold was also found as the direct result of your information. It was you who told Major Pidcock in the ambulance about the seven sacks."

"I never said anything about seven sacks."

This falsehood was a master-stroke, for only half a sack had been found. She had not written this down. There was only the word of Pidcock and me to vouch for it, while against us stood her denial; and the actual quantity of gold.

"I have no further questions," said Rocklin.

"But I have," said Jenks. And then he

made the most of Mrs. Sproud, although many in the room were laughing, and she herself, I think, felt she had done little but sacrifice her own character without repairing the injury she had done black curly. Jenks made her repeat that she was frightened; not calm enough to be sure of voices, especially many speaking together; that she had seen no one throughout. He even attempted to show that the talk about the hay-stack might have been purely about hay, and that the half-sack of gold might have been put there at another time—might belong to some honest man this very moment.

"Did you ever know the young man who boarded with you to do a dishonorable thing?" inquired Jenks. "Did you not have the highest opinion of him?"

She had not expected a question like this. It nearly broke the woman down. She put her hand to her breast, and seemed afraid to trust her voice. "I have the highest opinion of him," she said, word painfully following word. "He—he used to know that."

"I have finished," said Jenks.

"Can I go?" asked the witness, and the attorneys bowed. She stood one hesitating moment in the witness-stand, and she looked at the jury and the court; then, as if almost in dread, she let her eyes travel to black curly. But his eyes were sullenly averted. Then Mrs. Sproud slowly made her way through the room, with one of the saddest faces I have ever seen, and the door closed behind her.

CHAPTER IX

We finished our case with all the prisoners identified, and some of them doubly. The defence was scarcely more than a sham. The flimsy alibis were destroyed even by the incompetent, unready Rocklin, and when the charge came blackness fell upon the citizens of Tucson. The judge's cold statements struck them as partisan, and they murmured and looked darkly at him. But the jury, with its Meakums, wore no expression at all during any of his remarks. Their eyes were upon him, but entirely fish-like. He dismissed the cumbersome futilities one by one. "Now three witnesses have between them recognized all the prisoners but one," he continued. "That one, a reputed pauper, paid several hundred dollars of debts in gold the morning after the robbery. The money is said to be the proceeds of a cattle sale. No cattle have ever been known to belong to this man, and the purchaser had never been known to have any income until this trial began. The prisoner's name was on Mrs. Sproud's paper. The statement of one witness that he sat on a stone and saw three other of the prisoners firing has been contradicted by a woman who described herself as having run away at once; it is supported by two men who are admitted by all to have remained, and in consequence been shot. Their statements have been assailed by no one. Their testimony stands on the record unimpeached. They have identified five prisoners. If you believe them—and remember that not a word they said has been questioned—" here the judge emphasized more and more clearly. He concluded with the various alternatives of fact according to which the jury must find its several possible verdicts. When he had finished, the room sat sullen and still, and the twelve went out. I am told that they remained ten minutes away. It seemed one to me.

When they had resumed their seats I noticed the same fishlike oracular eye in most of them unchanged. "Not guilty," said the foreman.

"What!" shouted the judge, startled out of all judicial propriety. "None of 'em?"

"Not guilty," monotonously repeated the foreman.

We were silent amid the din of triumph now raised by Tucson. In the laughter, the hand-shaking, the shouting, and the jubilant pistol-shots that some particularly free spirit fired in the old Cathedral Square, we went to our dinner; and not even Stirling could joke. "There's a certain natural justice done here in spite of them," he said. "They are not one cent richer for all their looted twenty-eight thousand. They come out free, but penniless."

·"How about Jenks and that jury?" said I. And Stirling shrugged his shoulders.

But we had yet some crowning impudence to learn. Later, in the street, the officers and I met the prisoners, their witnesses, and their counsel emerging from a photographer's studio. The Territorial Delegate had been taken in a group with his acquitted thieves. The Bishop had declined to be in this souvenir.

"That's a picture I want," said I. "Only I'll be sorry to see your face there," I added to black curly.

"Indeed!" put in Jenks.

"Yes," said I. "You and he do not belong in the same class. By-the-way, Mr. Jenks, I suppose you'll return their horses and saddles now?"

Too many were listening for him to lose his temper, and he did a sharp thing. He took this public opportunity for breaking some news to his clients. "I had hoped to," he said; "that is, as many as were not needed to defray necessary costs. But it's been an expensive suit, and I've found myself obliged to sell them all. It's little enough to pay for clearing your character, boys."

They saw through his perfidy to them, and that he had them checkmated. Any protest from them would be a confession of their theft. Yet it seemed an unsafe piece of villainy in Jenks.

"They look disappointed," I remarked. "I shall value the picture very highly."

"If that's Eastern sarcasm," said Jenks, "it's beyond me."

"No, Mr. Jenks," I answered. "In your presence sarcasm drops dead. I think you'll prosper in politics."

But there I was wrong. There is some natural justice in these events, though I wish there were more. The jury, it is true, soon seemed oddly prosperous, as Stirling wrote me afterwards. They painted their houses; two of them, who had generally walked before, now had wagons; and in so many of their gardens and small ranches did the plants and fruits increase that, as Stirling put it, they had evidently sowed their dollars. But upon Jenks Territorial displeasure did descend. He had stayed away too much from Washington. A pamphlet appeared with the title, "What Luke Jenks Has Done for Arizona." Inside were twenty blank pages, and he failed of re-election.

Furthermore, the government retaliated upon this district by abandoning Camp Thomas and Lowell Barracks, those important sources of revenue for the neighborhood. The brief boom did not help Tucson very long, and left it poorer than ever.

At the station I saw Mrs. Sproud and black curly, neither speaking to the other. It was plain that he had utterly done with her, and that she was too proud even to look at him. She went West, and he as far east as Willcox. Neither one have I ever seen again.

But I have the photograph, and I sometimes wonder what has happened to black curly. Arizona is still a Territory; and when I think of the Gila Valley and of the Boy Orator, I recall Bishop Meakum's remark about our statesmen at Washington: "You can divide them birds in two lots—those who know better, and those who don't. D'you follow me?"

La Tinaja Bonita

"And it came to pass after a while that the brook dried up, because there had been no rain in the land."
                                    —*I Kings xvii. 7.*

CHAPTER I

A pretty girl was kneeling on the roof of a flat mud cabin, a harvest of red peppers round her knees. On the ground below her stood a swarthy young man, the bloom on his Mexican cheeks rich and dusky, like her own. His face was irresponsible and winning, and his watching eyes shone upon her with admiration and desire. She on the roof was entertained by her visitor's attention, but unfavorable to it. Through the livelong sunny day she had parried his love-talk with light and complete skill, enjoying herself, and liking him very well, as she had done since they were two children playing together in the Arizona desert. She was quite mistress of the situation, because she was a woman, and he as yet merely a boy; he was only twenty-two; she was almost sixteen. The Mexican man at twenty-two may be as experienced as his Northern brother of thirty, but at sixteen the Mexican woman is also mature, and can competently deal with the man. So this girl had relished the thoughtless morning and noon as they passed; but twice lately she had glanced across the low tree-tops of her garden down the trail, where the cañon descended to the silent plain below.

"I think I must go back now," said the young man, not thinking so. He had a guitar from the cabin.

"Oh!" said she, diverted by his youthful feint. "Well, if you think it is so late." She busied herself with the harvest. Her red handkerchief and strands of her black hair had fallen loosely together from her head to her shoulders. The red peppers were heaped thick, hiding the whole roof, and she stooped among them, levelling them to a ripening layer with buckskin gloves (for peppers sting sharper than mustard), sorting and turning them in the bright sun. The boy looked at her most wistfully.

"It is not precisely late—yet," said he.

"To be sure not," she assented, consulting the sky. "We have still three hours of day."

He brightened as he lounged against a

water-barrel. "But after night it is so very dark on the trail to camp," he insincerely objected.

"I never could have believed you were afraid of the dark."

"It is for the horse's legs, Lolita. Of course I fear nothing."

"Bueno! I was sure of it. Do you know, Luis, you have become a man quite suddenly? That mustache will be beautiful in a few years. And you have a good figure."

"I am much heavier than last year," said he. "My arm—"

"I can see, I can see. I am not sure I shall let you kiss me any more. You didn't offer to when you came this morning—and that shows you men perceive things more quickly than we can. But don't go yet. You can lead your horse. His legs will come to no harm, eased of your weight. I should have been lonely to-day, and you have made it pass so quickly. You have talked so much that my peppers are not half spread."

"We could finish them in five minutes together," said the youth, taking a step.

"Two up here among all these peppers! Oh no, Luis. We should tread on them, and our ankles would burn all night. If you want to help me, go bring some fresh water. The barrel is almost empty."

But Luis stood ardently gazing up at the roof.

"Very well, then," said Lolita. "If you like this better, finish the peppers, and I'll go for the water."

"Why do you look down the trail so often?" said the baffled love-maker, petulantly.

"Because Uncle Ramon said the American would be coming to-day," the girl replied, softly.

"Was it Uncle Ramon said that? He told you that?"

"Why not?" She shaded her eyes, and looked where the cañon's widening slit gave view of a slant of sand merging fan-spread into a changeless waste of plain. Many watercourses, crooked and straight, came out of the gaps, creasing the sudden Sierra, descending to the flat through bushes and leaning margin trees; but in these empty shapes not a rill tinkled to refresh the silence, nor did a drop slide over the glaring rocks, or even dampen the heated, cheating sand. Lolita strained her gaze at the dry distance, and stooped again to her harvest.

"What does he come here for?" demanded Luis.

"The American? We buy white flour of him sometimes."

"Sometimes! That must be worth his while! He will get rich!" Luis lounged back against his water-barrel, and was silent. As he watched Lolita, serenely working, his silver crescent ear-rings swung a little with the slight tilting of his head, and his fingers, forgotten and unguided by his thoughts, ruffled the strings of the guitar, drawing from it gay, purposeless tendrils of sound. Occasionally, when Lolita knew the song, she would hum it on the roof, inattentively, busy rolling her peppers:

" 'Soy purita mejicana;
    Nada tengo español.' "

(I am a pure Mexican. I have nothing Spanish about me.) And this melodious inattention of Lolita's Luis felt to be the extreme of slight.

"Have you seen him lately?" he asked, sourly.

"Not very. Not since the last time he came to the mines from Maricopa."

"I heard a man at Gun Sight say he was dead," snapped Luis.

But she made no sign. "That would be a pity," she said, humming gayly.

"Very sad. Uncle Ramon would have to go himself to Maricopa for that white flour."

Pleased with this remark, the youth took to song himself; and there they were like two mischievous birds. Only the bird on the ground was cross with a sense of failure. "El telele se murió," he sang.

" 'The hunchback is dead.
  Ay! Ay! Ay!
  And no one could be found to bury him
    except—' "

"Luis, aren't you going to get my water
for me?"

"Poco tiempo: I'll bring it directly."

"You have to go to the Tinaja Bonita for
it."

The Pretty Spring—or water-hole, or
tank—was half a mile from the cabin.

"Well, it's not nice out there in the sun. I
like it better in here, where it is pleasant.

" 'And no one could be found to bury him
    except
  Five dragoons and a corporal
  And the sacristan's cat.' "

Singing resentfully, young Luis stayed in
here, where it was pleasant. Bright green
branches of fruit-trees and small cotton-
woods and a fenced irrigated square of
green growing garden hid the tiny adobe
home like a nut, smooth and hard and dry
in their clustered midst. The lightest air
that could blow among these limber, ready
leaves set going at once their varnished
twinkling round the house. Their white and
dark sides gleamed and went out with chas-
ing lights that quickened the torpid place

114

into a holiday of motion. Closed in by this cool green, you did not have to see or think of Arizona, just outside.

"Where is Uncle Ramon to-day?" inquired Luis, dropping his music.

She sighed. "He has gone to drive our cattle to a new spring. There is no pasture at the Tinaja Bonita. Our streams and ditches went dry last week. They have never done so in all the years before. I don't know what is going to happen to us." The anxiety in the girl's face seemed to come outward more plainly for a moment, and then recede to its permanent abiding-place.

"There cannot be much water to keep flour-sellers alive on the trail to Maricopa," chirped the bird on the ground.

She made no answer to this. "What are you doing nowadays?" she asked.

"I have been working very hard on the wood contract for the American soldiers," he replied, promptly.

"By Tucson?"

"No. Huachuca."

"Away over there again? I thought you had cut all they wanted last May."

"It is of that enterprise of which I speak, Lolita."

"But it's October now!" Lolita lifted her face, ruddy with stooping, and broke into laughter.

"I do not see why you mock me. No one has asked me to work since."

"Have you asked any one for work?"

"It is not my way to beg."

"Luis, I don't believe you're quite a man yet, in spite of your mustache. You complain there's no money for Mexicans in Arizona because the Americans get it all. Why don't you go back to Sonora, then, and be rich in five minutes? It would sound finely: 'Luis Romero, Merchant, Hermosillo.' Or perhaps gold would fall more quickly into your lap at Guaymas. You would live in a big house, perhaps with two stories, and I would come and visit you at Easter—if your wife would allow it." Here Lolita threw a pepper at him.

The guitar grated a few pretty notes; otherwise there was silence.

"And it was Uncle Ramon persuaded them to hire you in May. He told the American contractor you owned a strong burro good for heavy loads. He didn't say much about you," added the little lady.

"Much good it did me! The American contractor-pig retained my wages to pay for the food he supplied us. They charge you extra for starvation, those gringos. They are all pigs. Ah, Lolita, a man needs a wife, so he may strive to win a home for her."

"I have heard men say that they needed a

116

home before they could strive to win a wife for it. But you go about it the other way."

"I am not an American pig, I thank the Virgin! I have none of their gringo customs."

"You speak truly indeed," murmured Lolita.

"It is you who know about them," the boy said, angry like a child. He had seen her eye drawn to the trail again as by a magnet. "They say you prefer gringos to your own people."

"Who dares say that?"

The elated Luis played loudly on the guitar. He had touched her that time.

But Lolita's eye softened at the instant of speaking, and she broke into her sweet laugh. "There!" she said, recapturing the situation; "is it not like old times for you and me to be fighting."

"Me? I am not fighting."

"You relieve me."

"I do not consider a gringo worth my notice."

"Sensible boy! You speak as wisely as one who has been to school in a large city. Luis, do you remember the day Uncle Ramon locked me up for riding on the kicking burro, and you came and unlocked me when uncle was gone? You took me walking, and lost us both in the mountains. We were really only a little, little way from home, but I thought we had got into another country where they eat children. I was six, and I beat you for losing me, and cried, and you were big, and you kissed me till I stopped crying. Do you remember?"

"No."

"Don't you remember?"

"I don't remember child's tricks."

"Luis, I have come to a conclusion. You are still young enough for me to kiss quite safely. Every time you fight with me—I shall kiss you. Won't you get me some fresh water now?"

He lounged, sulky, against his barrel.

"Come, querido! Must I go all that way myself? Well, then, if you intend to stand and glare at me till the moon rises— Ah! he moves!"

Luis laid the guitar gradually down, and gradually lifting a pail in which the dipper rattled with emptiness, he proceeded to crawl on his journey.

"You know that is not the one we use, muchacho," (little boy), remarked Lolita.

"Keep your kisses for your gringo," the water-carrier growled, with his back to her.

"I shall always save some for my little cousin."

The pail clattered on the stones, and the child stopped crawling. She on the roof stared at this performance for an open-mouthed moment, gloves idle among the spicy peppers. Then, laughing, she sprang to her feet, descended, and, catching up the water-jar (the olla de agua), overtook him, and shook it in his face with the sweetest derision. "Now we'll go together," said she, and started gayly through the green trees and the garden. He followed her, two paces behind, half ashamed, and gazing at her red handkerchief, and the black hair blowing a little; thus did they cross the tiny cool home acre through the twinkling pleasantness of the leaves, and pass at once outside the magic circle of irrigation into Arizona's domain, among a prone herd of carcasses upon the ground—dead cattle, two seasons dead now, hunted to this sanctuary by the drought, killed in the sanctuary by cold water.

CHAPTER II

A wise, quiet man, with a man's will, may sometimes after three days of thirst still hold grip enough upon his slipping mind to know, when he has found the water, that he must not drink it, must only dampen his lips and tongue in a drop-by-drop fashion until he has endured the passing of many slow, insidious hours. Even a wise man had best have a friend by his side then, who shall fight and tear him from the perilous excesses that he craves, knock him senseless if he cannot pin him down; but cattle know nothing of drop by drop, and you cannot pin down a hundred head that have found water after three days. So these hundred had drunk themselves swollen, and died. Cracked hide and white bone they lay, brown, dry, gaping humps straddled stiff askew in the last convulsion; and over them presided Arizona—silent, vast, all sunshine everlasting.

Luis saw these corpses that had stumbled to their fate, and he remembered; with Lolita in those trees all day, he had forgotten for a while. He pointed to the wide-strewn sight, familiar, monotonous as misfortune. "There will be many more," he said. "Another rainy season is gone without doing anything for the country. It cannot rain now for another year, Lolita."

"God help us and our cattle, and travellers!" she whispered.

Luis musingly repeated a saying of the country about the Tinaja Bonita,

" 'When you see the Black Cross dry,
   Fill the wagon cisterns high' "

—a doggerel in homely Spanish metre, unwritten mouth-to-mouth wisdom, stable as a proverb, enduring through generations of unrecorded wanderers, that repeated it for a few years, and passed beneath the desert.

"But the Black Cross has never been dry yet," Luis said.

"You have not seen it lately," said Lolita.

"Lolita! do you mean—" He looked in her troubled eyes, and they went on in silence together. They left behind them the bones and the bald level on which they lay, and came to where the cañon's broader descent quickened until they sank below that sight of the cattle, and for a time below the home and trees. They went down steeply by cactus and dry rock to a meeting of several cañons opening from side rifts in the Sierra, furrowing the main valley's mesa with deep watercourses that brought no water. Finding their way in this lumpy meeting-ground, they came upon the lurking-place of the Tinaja Bonita. They stood above it at the edge of a pitch of rock, watching the motionless crystal of the pool.

"How well it hides down there in its own cañon!" said Luis. "How pretty and clear! But there's plenty of water, Lolita."

"Can you see the Black Cross?"

"Not from here."

They began descending around the sides of the crumbled slate-rock face that tilted too steep for foothold.

"The other well is dry, of course," said Lolita. In the slaty, many-ledged formation a little lower down the cañon, towards the peep of outlying open country which the cloven hills let in, was a second round hole, twin of the first. Except after storms, water was never in this place, and it lay dry as a kiln nine-tenths of the year. But in size and depth and color, and the circular fashion of

123

its shaft, which seemed man's rather than nature's design, it might have been the real Tinaja's reflection, conjured in some evil mirror where everything was faithfully represented except the water.

"It must have been a real well once," said Luis.

"Once, yes."

"And what made it go dry?"

"Who knows?"

"How strange it should be the lower well that failed, Lolita!"

The boy and girl were climbing down slowly, drawing near each other as they reached the bottom of the hollow. The peep of open country was blocked, and the tall tops of the mountains were all of the outer world to be seen down here below the mesa's level. The silence was like something older than this world, like the silence of space before any worlds were made.

"Do you believe it ever can go dry?" asked Luis. They were now on the edge of the Tinaja.

"Father Rafael says that it is miraculous," said the girl, believingly.

Opposite, and everywhere except where they were, the walls went sheer down, not slate-colored, but white, with a sudden up-cropping formation of brick-shaped stones. These also were many-layered and crumbling, cracking off into the pool if the hand hung or the foot weighed on them. No safe way went to the water but at this lower side, where the riven, tumbled white blocks shelved easily to the bottom; and Luis and Lolita looked down these natural stairs at the portent in the well. In that white formation shot up from the earth's bowels, arbitrary and irrelevant amid the surrounding alien layers of slate, four black stones were lodged as if built into the wall by some hand—four small stones shaping a cross, back against the white, symmetrical and plain.

"It has come farther—more uncovered since yesterday," Lolita whispered.

"Can the Tinaja sink altogether?" repeated Luis. The arms of the cross were a measurable space above the water-line, and he had always seen it entirely submerged.

"How could it sink?" said Lolita, simply. "It will stop when the black stones are wholly dry."

"You believe Father Rafael," Luis said, always in a low voice; "but it was only Indians, after all, who told the mission fathers at the first."

"That was very long ago," said she, "and there has always been water in the Tinaja Bonita."

Boy and girl had set the jar down, and forgotten it and why they had come. Luis looked uneasily at the circular pool, and up from this creviced middle of the cañon to the small high tops of the mountains rising in the free sky.

"This is an evil place," he said. "As for the water—no one, no three, can live long enough to be sure."

But it was part of Lolita's religion. "I am sure," said she.

The young Mexican's eyes rested on the face of the girl beside him, more beautiful just then with some wave of secret fear and faith.

"Come away with me, Lolita!" he pleaded, suddenly. "I can work. I can be a man. It is fearful for you to live here alone."

"Alone, Luis?" His voice had called her from her reverie back to her gay, alert self. "Do you consider Uncle Ramon nobody to live with?"

"Yes. Nobody—for you."

"Promise me never to tell that to uncle. He is so considerate that he might make me marry somebody for company. And then, you know, my husband would be certain to be stupid about your coming to see me, querido."

"Why do you always mock me, Lolita?"

"Mock? What a fancy! Oh, see how the sun's going! If we do not get our water, your terrible Tinaja will go dry before supper. Come, Luis, I carried the olla. Must I do everything?"

He looked at her disconsolate. "Ah!" he vibrated, revelling in deep imaginary passion.

"Go! go!" she cried, pushing him. "Take your olla."

Upon the lightest passing puff of sentiment the Southern breast can heave with every genuine symptom of storm, except wreck. Of course she stirred his gregarious heart. Was she not lovely and he twenty-two? He went down the natural stairs and came slowly up with the water, stopping a step below her. "Lolita," he said, "don't you love me at all? not a very little?"

"You are my dearest, oldest friend, Luis," she said, looking at him with such full sweetness that his eyes fell. "But why do you pretend five beans makes ten?"

"Of course they only make ten with gringos."

She held up a warning finger.

"Oh yes, oh yes! Strangers make fine lovers!" With this he swelled to a fond, dangerous appearance, and muttered, "It is not difficult to kill a man, Lolita."

"Fighting! after what I told you!" Lolita stooped and kissed her cousin Luis, and he instantly made the most of that chance.

"As often as you please," he said, as she released herself angrily, and then a stroke of sound struck their two hearts still. They jumped apart, trembling. Some of the rock slide had rattled down and plunged into the Tinaja with a gulping resonance. Loitering strings of sand strewed after it, and the boy's and girl's superstitious eyes looked up from the ringed, waving water to the ledge. Lolita's single shriek of terror turned to joy as she uttered it.

"I thought—I thought you would not come!" she cried out.

The dismounted horseman above made no sign of understanding her words. He stepped carefully away from the ledge his foot had crumbled, and they saw him using his rifle like a staff, steadying its stock in successive niches, and so working back to his horse. There he slid the rifle into its leather sling along the left side of his saddle.

"So he is not dead," murmured Luis, "and we need not live alone."

"Come down!" the girl called, and waved her hand. But the new-comer stood by his horse like an apparition.

"Perhaps he is dead, after all," Luis said. "You might say some of the Mass, only he was a heretic. But his horse is Mexican, and a believer."

Lolita had no eyes or ears for Luis any more. He prattled away on the stone stairs of the Tinaja, flippant after a piercing shock of fear. To him, unstrung by the silence and the Black Cross and the presence of the sinking pool, the stone had crashed like a clap of sorcery, and he had started and stared to see—not a spirit, but a man, dismounted from his horse, with a rifle. At that his heart clutched him like talons, and in the flashing spasm of his mind came a picture—smoke from the rifle, and himself bleeding in the dust. Costly love-making! For Luis did not believe the rifle to have been brought to the ledge there as a staff, and he thanked the Virgin for the stone that fell and frightened him, and made him move suddenly. He had chattered himself cool now, and ready. Lolita was smiling at the man on the hill, glowing without concealment of her heart's desire.

"Come down!" she repeated. "Come round the side." And, lifting the olla, she tapped it, and signed the way to him.

"He has probably brought too much white flour for Uncle Ramon to care to climb more than he must," said Luis. But the man had stirred at last from his sentinel stillness, and began leading his horse down. Presently he was near enough for Luis to read his face. "Your gringo is a handsome fellow, certainly," he commented. "But he does not like me to-day."

"Like you! He doesn't think about you," said Lolita.

"Ha! That's your opinion?"

"It is also his opinion—if you'll ask him."

"He is afraid of Cousin Luis," stated the youth.

"Cousin grasshopper! He could eat you—if he could see you."

"There are other things in this world besides brute muscle, Lolita. Your gringo thinks I am worth notice, if you do not."

"How little he knows you!"

"It is you he does not know very well," the boy said, with a pang.

The scornful girl stared.

"Oh, the innocent one!" sneered Luis. "Grasshopper, indeed! Well, one man can always recognize another, and the women don't know much."

But Lolita had run off to meet her chosen lover. She did not stop to read his face. He was here; and as she hurried towards him she had no thought except that he was come at last. She saw his eyes and lips, and to her they were only the eyes and lips that she had longed for. "You have come just in time," she called out to him. At the voice, he looked at her one instant, and looked away; but the nearer sight of her sent a tide of scarlet across his face. His actions he could control, his bearing, and the steadiness of his speech, but not the coursing of his blood. It must have been a minute he had stood on the ledge above, getting a grip of himself. "Luis was becoming really afraid that he might have to do some work," continued Lolita, coming up the stony hill. "You know Luis?"

"I know him."

"You can fill your two canteens and carry the olla for us," she pursued, arriving eagerly beside him, her face lifted to her strong, tall lover.

"I can."

At this second chill of his voice, and his way of meeting her when she had come running, she looked at him bewildered, and the smile fluttered on her lips and left them. She walked beside him, talking no more; nor could she see his furtive other hand mutely open and shut, helping him keep his grip.

Luis also looked at the man who had taken Lolita's thoughts away from him and all other men. "No, indeed, he does not understand her very well," he repeated, bitter in knowing the man's suspicion and its needlessness. Something—disappointment, it may be—had wrought more reality in the young Mexican's easy-going love. "And she likes this gringo because—because he is light-colored!" he said, watching the American's bronzed Saxon face, almost as young as his own, but of sterner stuff. Its look left him no further doubt, and he held himself forewarned. The American came to the bottom, powerful, blue-eyed, his mustache golden, his cheek clean-cut, and beaten to shining health by the weather. He swung his blue-overalled leg over his saddle and rode to the Tinaja, with a short greeting to the watcher, while the pale Lolita unclasped the canteen straps and brought the water herself, brushing coldly by Luis to hook the canteens to the saddle again. This slighting touch changed the Mexican boy's temper to diversion and malice. Here were mountains from mole-hills! Here were five beans making ten with a vengeance!

"Give me that," said the American; and Luis handed up the water-jar to him with such feline politeness that the American's blue eyes filled with fire and rested on him for a doubtful second. But Luis was quite ready, and more diverted than ever over the suppressed violence of his Saxon friend. The horseman wheeled at once, and took a smooth trail out to the top of the mesa, the girl and boy following.

As the three went silent up the cañon, Luis caught sight of Lolita's eyes shining with the hurt of her lover's rebuff, and his face sparkled with further mischief. "She has been despising me all day," he said to himself. "Very well, very well.—Señor Don Ruz," he began aloud, elaborately, "we are having a bad drought."

The American rode on, inspecting the country.

"I know at least four sorts of kisses," reflected the Mexican trifler. "But there! very likely to me also they would appear alike from the top of a rock." He looked the American over, the rifle under his leg, his pistol, and his knife. "How clumsy these gringos are when it's about a girl!" thought Luis. "Any fool could fool them. Now I should take much care to be friendly if ever I did want to kill a man in earnest. Comical gringo!—Yes, very dry weather, Don Ruz. And the rainy season gone!"

The American continued to inspect the country, his supple, flannel-shirted back hinting no interest in the talk.

"Water is getting scarce, Don Ruz," persisted the gadfly, lighting again. "Don Ramon's spring does not run now, and so we must come to the Tinaja Bonita, you see. Don Ramon removed the cattle yesterday. Everybody absent from home, except Lolita." Luis thought he could see his Don Ruz listening to that last piece of gossip, and his smile over himself and his skill grew more engaging. "Lolita has been telling me all today that even the Tinaja will go dry."

"It was you said that!" exclaimed the brooding, helpless Lolita.

"So I did. And it was you said no. Well, we found something to disagree about." The man in the flannel shirt was plainly attending to his tormentor. "No sabe cuantos son cinco," Luis whispered, stepping close to

Lolita. "Your gringo could not say boo to a goose just now." Lolita drew away from her cousin, and her lover happened to turn his head slightly, so that he caught sight of her drawing away. "But what do you say yourself, Don Ruz?" inquired Luis, pleased at this slight coincidence—"will the Tinaja go dry, do you think?"

"I expect guessing won't interfere with the water's movements much," finally remarked Don Ruz—Russ Genesmere. His drawl and the body in his voice were not much like the Mexican's light fluency. They were music to Lolita, and her gaze went to him once more, but he got no answer. The bitter Luis relished this too.

"You are right, Don Ruz. Guessing is idle. Yet how can we help wondering about this mysterious Tinaja? I am sure that you can never have seen so much of the cross out of water. Lolita says—"

"So that's that place," said Genesmere, roughly.

Luis looked inquiring.

"Down there," Genesmere explained, with a jerk of his head back along the road they had come.

Luis was surprised that Don Ruz, who knew this country so well, should never have seen the Tinaja Bonita until to-day.

"I'd have seen it if I'd had any use for it," said Genesmere.

"To be sure, it lay off the road of travel," Luis assented. And of course Don Ruz knew all that was needful—how to find it. He knew what people said—did he not? Father Rafael, Don Ramon, everybody? Lolita perhaps had told him? And that if the cross ever rose entirely above the water, that was a sign all other water-holes in the region were empty. Therefore it was a good warning for travellers, since by it they could judge how much water to carry on a journey. But certainly he and Lolita were surprised to see how low the Tinaja had fallen to-day. No doubt what the Indians said about the great underground snake that came and sucked all the wells dry in the lower country, and in consequence was nearly satisfied before he reached the Tinaja, was untrue.

To this tale of Jesuits and peons the American listened with unexpressed contempt, caring too little to mention that he had heard some of it before, or even to say that in the last few days he had crossed the desert from Tucson and found water on the trail as usual where he expected. He rode on, leading the way slowly up the cañon, suffering the glib Mexican to talk unanswered. His own suppressed feelings still smouldered in his eye, still now and then knotted the muscles in his cheeks; but of Luis's chatter he said his whole opinion in one word, a single English syllable, which he uttered quietly for his own benefit. It also benefited Luis. He was familiar with that order of English, and, overhearing, he understood. It consoled the Mexican to feel how easily he could play this simple, unskilful American.

CHAPTER III

They passed through the hundred corpses to the home and the green trees, where the sun was setting against the little shaking leaves.

"So you will camp here to-night, Don Ruz?" said Luis, perceiving the American's pack-mules. Genesmere had come over from the mines at Gun Sight, found the cabin empty, and followed Lolita's and her cousin's trail, until he had suddenly seen the two from that ledge above the Tinaja. "You are always welcome to what we have at our camp, you know, Don Ruz. All that is mine is yours also. To-night it is probably frijoles. But no doubt you have white flour here." He was giving his pony water from the barrel, and next he threw the saddle on and mounted. "I must be going back, or they will decide I am not coming till to-morrow, and quickly eat my supper." He spoke jauntily from his horse, arm akimbo, natty short jacket put on for to-day's court-ing, gray steeple-hat silver-embroidered, a spruce, pretty boy, not likely to toil se-verely at wood contracts so long as he could hold soul and body together and otherwise be merry, and the hand of that careless arm soft on his pistol, lest Don Ruz should abruptly dislike him too much; for Luis contrived a tone for his small-talk that would have disconcerted the most sluggish, sweet to his own mischievous ears, healing to his galled self-esteem. "Good-night, Don Ruz. Good-night, Lolita. Perhaps I shall come to-morrow, mañana en la mañana."

"Good-night," said Lolita, harshly, which increased his joy; "I cannot stop you from passing my house."

Genesmere said nothing, but sat still on his white horse, hands folded upon the horns of his saddle, and Luis, always engag-ing and at ease, ambled away with his song about the hunchback. He knew that the American was not the man to wait until his enemy's back was turned.

> " 'El telele se murió
>   A enterrar ya le llevan—' "

The tin-pan Mexican voice was empty of melody and full of rhythm.

" 'Ay! Ay! Ay!' "

Lolita and Genesmere stood as they had stood, not very near each other, looking after him and his gayety that the sun shone bright upon. The minstrel truly sparkled. His clothes were more elegant than the American's shirt and overalls, and his face luxuriant with thoughtlessness. Like most of his basking Southern breed, he had no visible means of support, and nothing could worry him for longer than three minutes. Frijoles do not come high, out-of-doors is good enough to sleep in if you or your friend have no roof, and it is not a hard thing to sell some other man's horses over the border and get a fine coat and hat.

" 'Cinco dragones y un cabo,
    Oh, no no no no no!
    Y un gato de sacristán.' "

Coat and hat were getting up the cañon's side among the cactus, the little horse climbing the trail shrewdly with his light-weight rider; and dusty, unmusical Genesmere and sullen Lolita watched them till they went behind a bend, and nothing remained but the tin-pan song singing in

Genesmere's brain. The gadfly had stung more poisonously than he knew, and still Lolita and Genesmere stood watching nothing, while the sun—the sun of Arizona at the day's transfigured immortal passing—became a crimson coal in a lake of saffron, burning and beating like a heart, till the desert seemed no longer dead, but only asleep, and breathing out wide rays of rainbow color that rose expanded over earth and sky.

Then Genesmere spoke his first volunteered word to Lolita. "I didn't shoot because I was afraid of hitting you," he said.

So now she too realized clearly. He had got off his horse above the Tinaja to kill Luis during that kiss. Complete innocence had made her stupid and slow.

"Are you going to eat?" she inquired.

"Oh yes. I guess I'll eat."

She set about the routine of fire-lighting and supper as if it had been Uncle Ramon, and this evening like all evenings. He, not so easily, and with small blunderings that he cursed, attended to his horse and mules, coming in at length to sit against the wall where she was cooking.

"It is getting dark," said Lolita. So he found the lamp and lighted it, and sat down again.

"I've never hurt a woman," he said, presently, the vision of his rifle's white front sight held steady on the two below the ledge once more flooding his brain. He spoke slowly.

"Then you have a good chance now," said Lolita, quickly, busy over her cooking. In her Southern ears such words sounded a threat. It was not in her blood to comprehend this Northern way of speaking and walking and sitting, and being one thing outside and another inside.

"And I wouldn't hurt a woman"—he was hardly talking to her—"not if I could think in time."

"Men do it," she said, with the same defiance. "But it makes talk."

"Talk's nothing to me," said Genesmere, flaming to fierceness. "Do I care for opinions? Only my own." The fierceness passed from his face, and he was remote from her again. Again he fell to musing aloud, changing from Mexican to his mother-tongue. "I wouldn't want to have to remember a thing like that." He stretched himself, and leaned his elbows on his knees and his head in his hands, the yellow hair hiding his fingers. She had often seen him do this when he felt lazy; it was not a sign by which she could read a spiritual standstill, a quivering wreck of faith and passion. "I have to live a heap of my life alone," the lounger went on. "Journey alone. Camp alone. Me and my mules. And I don't propose to have thoughts a man should be ashamed of." Lolita was throwing a cloth over the table and straightening it. "I'm twenty-five, and I've laid by no such thoughts yet. Church folks might say different."

"It is ready," said Lolita, finishing her preparations.

He looked up, and, seeing the cloth and the places set, pulled his chair to the table, and passively took the food she brought him. She moved about the room between shelves and fire, and, when she had served him, seated herself at leisure to begin her own supper. Uncle Ramon was a peon of some substance, doing business in towns and living comparatively well. Besides the shredded spiced stew of meat, there were several dishes for supper. Genesmere ate the meal deliberately, attending to his plate and cup, and Lolita was as silent as himself, only occasionally looking at him; and in time his thoughts came to the surface again in words. He turned and addressed Lolita in Mexican: "So, you see, you saved his life down there."

She laid her fork down and gave a laugh, hard and harsh; and she said nothing, but waited for what next.

"You don't believe that. You don't know that. He knows that."

She laughed again, more briefly.

"You can tell him so. From me."

Replies seemed to struggle together on Lolita's lips and hinder each other's escaping.

"And you can tell him another thing. He wouldn't have stopped. He'd have shot. Say that. From me. He'd have shot, because he's a Spaniard, like you."

"You lie!" This side issue in some manner set free the girl's tongue, "I am not Spanish. I care nothing for Spaniards or what they may do. I am Mexican, and I waited to see you kill him. I wanted to watch his blood. But you! you listened to his false talk, and believed him, and let him go. I save his life? Go after him now! Do it with this knife, and tell him it is Lolita's. But do not sit there and talk any more. I have had enough of men's talk to-day. Enough, enough, enough!"

Genesmere remained in his chair, while she had risen to her feet. "I suppose," he said, very slowly, "that folks like you folks can't understand about love—not about the kind I mean."

Lolita's two hands clinched the edge of the table, and she called upon her gods. "Believe it, then! Believe it! And kill me, if that will make you contented. But do not talk any more. Yes, he told me that he loved me. Yes, I kissed him; I have kissed him hundreds of times, always, since before I can remember. And I had been laughing at

143

him to-day, having nothing in my heart but you. All day it had rejoiced me to hear his folly and think of you, and think how little he knew, and how you would come soon. But your folly is worse. Kill me in this house to-night, and I will tell you, dying, that I love you, and that it is you who are the fool."

She looked at her lover, and seeing his face and eyes she had sought to bring before her in the days that she had waited for him, she rushed to him.

"Lolita!" he whispered. "Lolita!"

But she could only sob as she felt his arms and his lips. And when presently he heard her voice again murmuring brokenly to him in the way that he knew and had said over in his mind and dwelt upon through the desert stages he had ridden, he trembled, and with savage triumph drew her close, and let his doubt and the thoughts that had chilled and changed him sink deep beneath the flood of this present rapture. "My life!" she said. "Toda mi vida! All my life!" Through the open door the air of the cañon blew cool into the little room overheated by the fire and the lamp, and in time they grew aware of the endless rustling of the trees, and went out and stood in the darkness together, until it ceased to be darkness, and their eyes could discern the near and distant shapes of their world. The sky was black and splendid, with four or five planets too bright for lesser stars to show, and the promontories of the keen mountains shone almost as in moonlight. A certain hill down towards the Tinaja and its slate ledge caught Genesmere's eye, and Lolita felt him shudder, and she wound her arm more tightly about him.

"What is it?" she said.

"Nothing." He was staring at the hill. "Nothing," he replied to himself.

"Dreamer, come!" said Lolita, pulling him. "It is cold here in the night—and if you choose to forget, I choose you shall remember."

"What does this girl want now?"

"The cards! our cards!"

"Why, to be sure!" He ran after her, and joy beat in her heart at the fleet kiss he tried for and half missed. She escaped into the room, laughing for delight at her lover's being himself again—his own right self that she talked with always in the long days she waited alone.

"Take it!" she cried out, putting the guitar at him so he should keep his distance. "There! now you have broken it, songless Americano! You shall buy me another." She flung the light instrument, that fell in a corner with a loud complaint of all the strings together, collapsing to a blurred hollow humming, and silence.

"Now you have done it!" said Genesmere, mock serious.

"I don't care. I am glad. He played on that to-day. He can have it, and you shall give me a new one.

" 'Yo soy purita mejicana;
    Nada tengo español,' "

sang the excited, breathless Lolita to her American, and seated herself at the table, beginning a brisk shuffle of a dim, dog-eared pack. "You sit there!" She nodded to the opposite side of the table. "Very well, move the lamp then." Genesmere had moved it because it hid her face from him. "He thinks I cheat! Now, Señor Don Ruz, it shall be for the guitar. Do you hear?"

"Too many pesos, señorita."

"Oh, oh! the miser!"

"I'm not going broke on any señoritas—not even my own girl!"

"Have you no newer thing than poverty to tell me? Now if you look at me like that I cannot shuffle properly."

"How am I to look, please?" He held his glance on her.

"Not foolish like a boy. There, take them, then!" She threw the cards at him, blushing and perturbed by his eyes, while he scrambled to punish her across the table.

"Generous one!" she said. "Ardent pretender! He won't let me shuffle because he fears to lose."

"You shall have a silk handkerchief with flowers on it," said he, shuffling.

"I have two already. I can see you arranging those cards, miser!"

It was the custom of their meetings, whether at the cabin or whether she stole out to his camp, to play for the token he should bring for her when he next came from town. She named one thing, he some other, and the cards judged between them. And to see Genesmere in these hours, his oldest friend could not have known him any more than he knew himself. Never had a woman been for him like Lolita, conjuring the Saxon to forget himself and bask openly in that Southern joy and laughter of the moment.

"Say my name!" he ordered; and at the child effort she made over "Russ" he smiled with delight. "Again!" he exclaimed, bending to catch her *R* and the whole odd little word she made. "More!"

"No," pouted the girl, and beat at him, blushing again.

"Make your bet!" he said, laying out the Mexican cards before him. "Quick! Which shall it be?"

"The caballo. Oh, my dear, I wanted to die this afternoon, and now I am so happy!"

It brought the tears to her eyes, and almost to his, till he suddenly declared she had stolen a card, and with that they came to soft blows and laughing again. So did the two sit and wrangle, seizing the pack out of turn, feigning rage at being cheated, until he juggled to make her win three times out of five; and when chance had thus settled for the guitar, they played for kisses, and so forgot the cards at last. And at last Genesmere began to speak of the next time, and Lolita to forbid such talk as that so soon. She laid her hand over his lips, at which he yielded for a little, and she improvised questions of moment to ask him, without time for stopping, until she saw that this would avail no longer. Then she sighed, and let him leave her to see to his animals, while she lighted the fire again to make breakfast for him. At that parting meal an anxiety slowly came in her face, and it was she that broke their silence after a while.

"Which road do you go this time, querido?" she asked.

"Tucson, Maricopa, and then straight here to you."

"From Maricopa? That is longer across the desert."

"Shorter to my girl."

"I—I wish you would not come that way."

"Why?"

"That—that desert!"

"There's desert both ways—all ways. The other road puts an extra week between you and me."

"Yes, yes. I have counted."

"What is all this, Lolita?"

Once more she hesitated, smiling uneasily beneath his scrutiny. "Yo no sé" (I don't know). "You will laugh. You do not believe the things that I believe. The Tinaja Bonita—"

"That again!"

"Yes," she half whispered. "I am afraid."

He looked at her steadily.

"Return the same road by Tucson," she urged. "That way is only half so much desert, and you can carry water from Poso Blanco. Do not trust the Coyote Wells. They are little and shallow, and if the Black Cross— Oh, my darling, if you do not believe, do this for me because you love me, love me!"

He did not speak at once. The two had risen, and stood by the open door, where the dawn was entering and mixing with the lamp. "Because I love you," he repeated at length, slowly, out of his uncertain thoughts.

She implored him, and he studied her in silence.

Suddenly hardness stamped his face. "I'll come by Tucson, then—since I love you!" And he walked at once out of the door. She followed him to his horse, and there reached up and pulled him round to her, locking her fingers behind his neck. Again his passion swept him, and burned the doubt from his eyes. "I believe you love me!" he broke out.

"Ah, why need you say that?"

"Adios, chiquita." He was smiling, and she looked at his white teeth and golden mustache. She felt his hands begin to unlock her own.

"Not yet—not yet!"

"Adios, chiquita."

"O mi querido!" she murmured; "with you I forget day and night!"

"Bastante!" He kissed her once for all.

"Good-bye! good-bye! Mis labios van estar fríos hasta que tu los toques otra vez" (My lips will be cold until you touch them again).

He caught her two hands, as if to cling to something. "Say that once more. Tell me that once more."

She told him with all her heart and soul, and he sprang into his saddle. She went beside him through the cold, pale-lighted trees to the garden's edge, and there stood while he took his way across the barren ground among the carcasses. She watched the tip of his mustache that came beyond the line of his cheek, and when he was farther, his whole strong figure, while the clack of the hoofs on the dead ground grew fainter. When the steeper fall of the cañon hid him from her she ran to the house, and from its roof among her peppers she saw him come into sight again below, the wide, foreshortened slant of ground between them, the white horse and dark rider and the mules, until they became a mere line of something moving, and so vanished into the increasing day.

CHAPTER IV

Genesmere rode, and took presently to smoking. Coming to a sandy place, he saw prints of feet and of a shod horse in the trail heading the other way. That was his own horse, and the feet were Lolita's and Luis's—the record and the memory of yesterday afternoon. He looked up from the trail to the hills, now lambent with violet and shifting orange, and their shapes as they moved out into his approaching view were the shapes of yesterday afternoon. He came soon to the forking of the trails, one for Tucson and the other leading down into the lumpy country, and here again were the prints in the sand, the shod horse, the man and the woman, coming in from the lumpy country that lay to the left; and Genesmere found himself stock-still by the forking trails, looking at his watch. His many-journeyed mules knew which was the Tucson trail, and, not understanding why he turned them from their routine, walked asunder, puzzled at being thus driven in the wrong direction. They went along a strange up-and-down path, loose with sliding stones, and came to an end at a ledge of slate, and stood about on the tricky footing looking at their master and leaning their heads together. The master sat quiet on his horse, staring down where a circular pool lay below; and the sun rose everywhere, except in his mind. So far had he come yesterday with that mind easy over his garnered prosperity, free and soaring on its daily flight among the towers of his hopes— those constructions that are common with men who grow fond: the air-castle rises and reaches, possessing the architect, who cherishes its slow creation with hourly changes and additions to the plan. A house was part of Genesmere's castle, a home with a wife inside, and no more camping alone. Thus far, to this exact ledge, the edifice had gone forward fortunately, and then a blast had crumbled house and days to come into indistinguishable dust. The heavy echo jarred in Genesmere, now that he had been lured to look again upon the site of the disaster, and a lightning violence crossed his face. He saw the two down there as they had stood, the man with his arms holding the woman, before the falling stone had startled them. Were the Mexican present now in the flesh, he would destroy him just for what he had tried to do. If she were true— She was true—that was no thanks to the Mexican. Genesmere was sorry second thoughts had spared that fellow yesterday, and he looked at his watch again. It was time to be starting on the Tucson trail, and the mules alertly turned their steps from the Tinaja Bonita. They could see no good in having come here. Evidently it was not to get water. Why, then? What use was there in looking down a place into a hole? The mules gave it up. Genesmere himself thought the Tinaja poorly named. It was not pretty. In his experience of trail and cañon he knew no other such hole. He was not aware of the twin, dried up, thirty yards below, and therefore only half knew the wonders of the spot.

He rode back to the forks across the rolling steepness, rebuilding the castle; then, discovering something too distant to be sure about, used his glass quickly. It was another rider, also moving slowly among the knolls and gullies of the mesa, and Genesmere could not make him out. He was going towards the cabin, but it was not the same horse that Luis had ridden yesterday. This proved nothing, and it would be easy to circle and see the man closer—only not worth the trouble. Let the Mexican go to the cabin. Let him go every day. He probably would, if she permitted. Most likely she would tell him to keep away from her. She ought to. She might hurt him if he annoyed her. She was a good shot with a pistol. But women work differently from men—and then she was Mexican. She might hide her feelings and make herself pleasant for three weeks. She would tell him when he returned, and they would laugh together over how she had fooled this Luis. After all, shooting would have been too much punishment. A man with a girl like Lolita must expect to find other men after her. It depends on your girl. You find that out when you go after other men's girls. When a woman surely loves some other man she will not look at you. And Lolita's love was a sure thing. A woman can say love and a man will believe her—until he has experienced the genuine article once; after that he can always tell. And to have a house, with her inside waiting for you! Such a turn was strange luck for a man, not to be accounted for. If anybody had said last year—why, as late as the 20th of last March—that settling down was what you were coming to—and now—Genesmere wondered how he could ever have seen anything in riding a horse up and down the earth and caring nothing for what next. "No longer alone!" he said aloud, suddenly, and surprised the white horse.

The song about the hunchback and the sacristan's cat stirred its rhythm in his mind. He was not a singer, but he could think the tune, trace it, naked of melody, in the dry realm of the brain. And it was a diversion to piece out the gait of the phantom notes, low after high, quick after slow, until they went of themselves. Lolita would never kiss Luis again; would never want to—not even as a joke. Genesmere turned his head back to take another look at the rider, and there stood the whole mountains like a picture, and himself far out in the flat country, and the bare sun in the sky. He had come six miles on the road since he had last noticed. Six miles, and the air-castle was rebuilt and perfect, with no difference from the old one except its foundation, which was upon sand. To see the unexpected plain around him, and the islands of blue, sharp peaks lying in it, drove the tune from his head, and he considered the well-known country, reflecting that man could not be meant to live here. The small mountain-islands lay at all distances, blue in a dozen ways, amid the dead calm of this sand archipelago. They rose singly from it, sheer

157

and sudden, toothed and triangled like ice-
bergs, hot as stoves. The channels to the
north, Santa Rosa way, opened broad and
yellow, and ended without shore upon the
clean horizon, and to the south narrowed
with lagoons into Sonora. Genesmere could
just see one top of the Sierra de la Quitabac
jutting up from below the earth-line, split-
ting the main channel, the faintest blue of
all. They could be having no trouble over
their water down there, with the Laguna
Esperanca and the Poso de Mazis. Genesmere killed some more of the way rehearsing the trails and water-holes of this
country, known to him like his pocket; and
by-and-by food-cooking and mule-feeding
and the small machine repetitions of a
camp and a journey brought the Quijotoa
Mountains behind him to replace Gun Sight
and the Sierra de la Naril; and later still the
Cababi hid the Quijotoa, and Genesmere
counted days and nights to the good, and
was at the Coyote Wells.

These were holes in rocks, but shallow,
as Lolita said. No shallower than ordinary,
however; he would see on the way back if
they gave signs of failing. No wonder if they
did, with this spell of drought—but why mix
up a plain thing with a lot of nonsense
about a black cross down a hole? Genesmere was critically struck with the words
of the tune he now noticed steadily running

in his head again, beneath the random surface of his thoughts.

> "Cinco dragones y un cabo,
>   Y un gato de sacristán."

That made no sense either; but Mexicans found something in it. Liked it. Now American songs had some sense:

> "They bathed his head in vinegar
>   To fetch him up to time,
> And now he drives a mule team on
>   The Denver City line."

A man could understand that. A proud stage-driver makes a mistake about a female passenger. Thinks he has got an heiress, and she turns out to peddle sarsaparilla. "So he's naturally used up," commented Genesmere. "You estimate a girl as one thing, and she—" Here the undercurrent welled up, breaking the surface. "Did she mean that? Was that her genuine reason?" In memory he took a look at his girl's face, and repeated her words when she besought him to come the longer way and hesitated over why. Was that shame at owning she believed such stuff? True, after asking him once about his religion and hearing what he said, she had never spoken of these things again. That must be a wom-

an's way when she loved you first—to hide
her notions that differed from yours, and
not ruffle happy days. "Return the same
road by Tucson!" He unwrapped a clean,
many-crumpled handkerchief, and held Lolita's photograph for a while. Then he burst
into an unhappy oath, and folded the picture up again. What if her priest did tell
her? He had heard the minister tell about
eternal punishment when he was a boy, and
just as soon as he started thinking it over
he knew it was a lie. And this quack Tinaja
was worse foolishness, and had nothing to
do with religion. Lolita afraid of his coming
to grief in a country he had travelled hundreds, thousands of miles in! Perhaps she
had never started thinking for herself yet.
But she had. She was smarter than any girl
of her age he had ever seen. She did not
want him back so soon. That was what it
was. Yet she had looked true; her voice had
sounded that way. Again he dwelt upon her
words and caresses; and harboring these
various thoughts, he killed still more of the
long road, until, passing after a while Poso
Blanco, and later Marsh's ranch-well at the
forks where the Sonora road comes in, he
reached Tucson a man divided against himself. Divided beyond his will into two
selves—one of faith besieged, and one of be-
sieging inimical reason—the inextricable
error!

Business and pleasure were waiting in Tucson, and friends whose ways and company had not been of late for him; but he frequented them this time, tasting no pleasure, yet finding the ways and company better than his own. After the desert's changeless, unfathomed silence, in which nothing new came day or night to break the fettering spell his mind was falling under, the clink and knocking of bottles was good to hear, and he listened for more, craving any sound that might liven or distract his haunted spirit. Instead of the sun and stars, here was a roof; instead of the pitiless clear air, here was tobacco smoke; and beneath his boot-heels a wooden floor wet with spilled liquids instead of the unwatered crumbling sand. Without drinking, he moved his chair near the noisiest drinkers, and thus among the tobacco smoke sought to hide from his own looming doubt. Later the purring tinkle of guitars reminded him of that promised present, and the next morning he was the owner of the best instrument that he could buy. Leaving it with a friend to keep until he should come through again from Maricopa, he departed that way with his mules, finding in the new place the same sort of friends and business, and by night looking upon the same untasted pleasures. He went about town with some cattlemen—carousing bankrupts, who

161

remembered their ruin in the middle of whiskey, and broke off to curse it and the times and climate, and their starved herds that none would buy at any price. Genesmere touched nothing, yet still drew his chair among these drinkers.

"Aren't you feeling good to-night, Russ?" asked one at length.

And Genesmere's eyes roused from seeing visions, and his ears became aware of the loud company. In Tucson he had been able to sit in the smoke, and compass a cheerful deceit of appearance even to himself. Choosing and buying the guitar had lent reality to his imitated peace of mind; he had been careful over its strings, selecting such as Lolita preferred, wrapt in carrying out this spiritual forgery of another Genesmere. But here they had noticed him; appearances had slipped from him. He listened to a piece of late Arizona news some one was in the middle of telling—the trial of several Mormons for robbing a paymaster near Cedar Springs. This was the fourth time he had heard the story, because it was new; but the present narrator dwelt upon the dodgings of a witness, a negress, who had seen everything and told nothing, outwitting the government, furnishing no proofs. This brought Genesmere quite back.

"No proofs!" he muttered. "No proofs!"

He laughed and became alert. "She lied to them good, did she?"

They looked at him, because he had not spoken for so long; and he was told that she had certainly lied good.

"Fooled them clean through, did she? On oath! Tell about her."

The flattered narrator, who had been in court, gave all he knew, and Genesmere received each morsel of perjury gravely with a nod. He sat still when the story was done.

"Yes," he said, after a time. "Yes." And again, "Yes." Then he briefly bade the boys good-night, and went out from the lamps and whiskey into the dark.

CHAPTER V

He walked up and down alone, round the
corral where his mules stood, round the
stable where his bed-blankets were; and one
or two carousers came by, who suggested
further enjoyments to him. He went to the
edge of the town and walked where passers
would not meet him, turning now and then
to look in the direction of Tucson, where
the guitar was waiting. When he felt the
change of dawn he went to the stable, and
by the first early gray had his mules packed.
He looked once again towards Tucson, and
took the road he had promised not to take,
leaving the guitar behind him altogether.
His faith protested a little, but the other self
invented a quibble, the mockery that he had

already "come by Tucson," according to his
literal word; and this device answered. It is
a comfort to be divided no longer against
one's self. Genesmere was at ease in his
thraldom to the demon with whom he had
wrestled through the dark hours. As the day
brightened he wondered how he had come
to fool a night away over a promise such as
that. He took out the face in the handkerchief, and gave it a curious, defiant smile.
She had said waiting would be long. She
should have him quickly. And he was going
to know about that visitor at the cabin, the
steeple-hatted man he saw in his visions. So
Maricopa drew behind him, small, clear-
grouped in the unheated morning, and the
sun found the united man and his mules
moving into the desert.

By the well in the bottom of the Santa
Cruz River he met with cattle and little late-
born calves trying to trot. Their mothers,
the foreman explained, had not milk enough
for them, nor the cursed country food or
water for the mothers. They could not chew
cactus. These animals had been driven here
to feed and fatten inexpensively, and get
quick money for the owner. But, instead,
half of them had died, and the men were
driving the rest to new pastures—as many,
that is, as could still walk. Genesmere
knew, the foreman supposed, that this well
was the last for more than a hundred miles?

Funny to call a thing like that Santa Cruz a river! Well, it was an Arizona river; all right enough, no doubt, somewhere a thousand feet or so underground. Pity you weren't a prairie-dog that eats sand when he gets a thirst on him. Got any tobacco? Good-bye.

Think of any valleys that you know between high mountains. Such was southern Arizona once—before we came. Then fill up your valleys with sand until the mountains show no feet or shoulders, but become as men buried to the neck. That is what makes separate islands of their protruding peaks, and that is why water slinks from the surface whenever it can and flows useless underneath, entombed in the original valley. This is Arizona now—since the pterodactyls have gone. In such a place the traveller turns mariner, only, instead of the stars, he studies the water-wells, shaping his course by these. Not sea-gulls, but ravens, fly over this waste, seeking their meal. Some were in front of Genesmere now, settled black in the recent trail of the cattle. He did not much care that the last well was gone by, for he was broken in by long travel to the water of the 'dobe-holes that people rely upon through this journey. These 'dobe-holes are occasional wallows in clayey spots, and men and cattle know each one. The cattle, of course, roll in them, and they become worn into circular hollows, their edges tramped into muck, and surrounded by a thicket belt of mesquite. The water is not good, but will save life. The first one lay two stages from the well, and Genesmere accordingly made an expected dry camp the first night, carrying water from the well in the Santa Cruz, and dribbling all of it but a cupful among his animals, and the second night reached his calculated 'dobe-hole. The animals rolled luxuriously in the brown, dungy mixture, and Genesmere made his coffee strong. He had had no shade at the first camp, and here it was good under the tangle of the mesquite, and he slept sound. He was early awakened by the ravens, whose loose, dislocated croaking came from where they sat at breakfast on the other side of the wallow. They had not suspected his presence among the mesquite, and when he stepped to the mud-hole and dipped its gummy fluid in his coffee-pot they rose hoarse and hovering, and flapped twenty yards away, and sat watching until he was gone into the desert, when they clouded back again round their carrion.

This day was over ground yellow and hard with dearth, until afternoon brought a footing of sifting sand heavy to travel in. He had plenty of time for thinking. His ease after the first snapping from his promise had changed to an eagerness to come unawares and catch the man in the steeple-hat.

Till that there could be no proofs. Genesmere had along the road nearly emptied his
second canteen of its brown-amber drink,
wetting the beasts' tongues more than his
own. The neighborhood of the next 'dobe-
hole might be known by the three miles of
cactus you went through before coming on
it, a wide-set plantation of the yucca. The
posted plants deployed over the plain in
strange extended order like legions and legions of figures, each shock-head of spears
bunched bristling at the top of its lank,
scaly stalk, and out of that stuck the
blossom-pole, a pigtail on end, with its knot
of bell-flowers seeded to pods ten feet in the
air. Genesmere's horse started and nearly
threw him, but it was only a young calf lying for shade by a yucca. Genesmere could
tell from its unlicked hide that the mother
had gone to hunt water, and been away for
some time. This unreasonable waif made a
try at running away, but fell in a heap, and
lay as man and mules passed on. Presently
he passed a sentinel cow. She stood among
the thorns guarding the calves of her sis-
ters till they should return from getting
their water. The desert cattle learn this
shift, and the sentinel now, at the stranger's
approach, lowered her head, and with a fee-
ble but hostile sound made ready to protect
her charge, keeping her face to the passing
enemy. Farther along gaunt cows stood or

lay under the perpetual yuccas, an animal
to every plant. They stared at Genesmere
passing on; some rose to look after him;
some lifted their heads from the ground,
and seeing, laid them down again. He came
upon a calf watching its mother, who had
fallen in such a position that the calf could
not suck. The cow's foreleg was caught over
her own head, and so she held herself from
rising. The sand was rolled and grooved
into a wheel by her circlings; her body
heaved and fell with breathing, and the
sand was wet where her pivot nostrils had
ground it. While Genesmere untangled her
and gave her tongue the last of his canteen
the calf walked round and round. He placed
the cow upon her feet, and as soon as he
moved away to his horse the calf came to
its mother, who began to lick it. He presently marked ahead the position of the coming 'dobe-hole by the ravens assembled in
the air, continually rising and lighting. The
white horse and mules quickened their step,
and the trail became obliterated by hundreds of hoof-marks leading to the water.
As a spider looks in the centre of an empty
web, so did the round wallow sit in the middle of the plain, with threaded feet con-
ducting from everywhere to it. Mules and
white horse scraped through the scratching
mesquite, and the ravens flapped up. To Genesmere their croaking seemed suddenly to

fill all space with loud total clamor, for no water was left, only mud. He eased the animals of their loads and saddles, and they rolled in the stiff mud, squeezing from it a faint ooze, and getting a sort of refreshment. Genesmere chewed the mud, and felt sorry for the beasts. He turned both canteens upsidedown and licked the bungs. A cow had had his last drink. Well, that would keep her alive several hours more. Hardly worth while; but spilled milk decidedly. Milk! That was an idea. He caught animal after animal, and got a few sickly drops. There was no gain in camping at this spot, no water for coffee; so Genesmere moved several hundred yards away to be rid of the ravens and their all-day-long meal and the smell. He lay thinking what to do. Go back? At the rate he could push the animals now that last hole might be used up by the cattle before he got there—and then it was two stages more to the Santa Cruz well. And the man would be gaining just so many more days unhindered at the cabin. Out of the question. Forward, it was one shortish drive to the next hole. If that were dry, he could forsake the trail and make a try by a short-cut for that Tinaja place. And he must start soon, too, as soon as the animals could stand it, and travel by night and rest when the sun got bad. What business had October to be hot like this? So in the darkness he mounted again, and noon found him with eyes shut under a yucca. It was here that he held a talk with Lolita. They were married, and sitting in a room with curtains that let you see flowers growing outside by the window, as he had always intended. Lolita said to him that there was no fool like an old fool, and he was telling her that love could make a man more a fool than age, when she threw the door open, letting in bright light, and said, "No proofs." The bright light was the real sun coming round the yucca on his face, and he sat up and saw the desert. No cows were here, but he noticed the roughened hides and sunk eyes of his own beasts, and spoke to them.

"Cheer up, Jeff! Stonewall!" He stopped at the pain. It was in his lips and mouth. He put up his hand, and the feel of his tongue frightened him. He looked round to see what country he was in, and noted the signs that it was not so very far now. The blue crags of the islands were showing, and the blue sterile sky spread over them and the ceaseless sunlight like a plague. Man and horse and mules were the only life in the naked bottom of this caldron. The mirage had caught the nearest island, and blunted and dissolved its points and frayed its base away to a transparent fringe.

"Like a lump of sugar melts in hot tod," remarked Genesmere, aloud, and remembered his thickened mouth again. "I can stand it off for a while yet, though—if they can travel." His mules looked at him when he came—looked when he tightened their cinches. "I know, Jeff," he said, and inspected the sky. "No heaven's up there. Nothing's back of that thing, unless it's hell."

He got the animals going, and the next 'dobe-hole was like the last, and busy with the black flapping of the birds. "You didn't fool me," said Genesmere, addressing the mud. "I knew you'd be dry." His eye ran over the cattle, that lay in various conditions. "That foreman was not too soon getting his live-stock out of your country," he continued to the hole, his tongue clacking as it made his words. "This live-stock here's not enjoying itself like its owners in town. This live-stock was intended for Eastern folks' dinner.—But you've got ahead of 'em this trip," he said to the ravens. He laughed loudly, and, hearing himself, stopped, and his face became stern. "You don't want to talk this way, Russ Genesmere. Shut your head. You're alone.—I wish I'd never known!" he suddenly cried out.

He went to his animals and sat down by them, clasping and unclasping his hands. The mules were lying down on the baked mud of the wallow with their loads on, and he loosed them. He stroked his white horse for some little while, thinking; and it was in his heart that he had brought these beasts into this scrape. It was sunset and cool. Against the divine fires of the west the peaks towered clear in splendor impassive, and forever aloof, and the universe seemed to fill with infinite sadness. "If she'll tell me it's not so," he said, "I'll believe her. I will believe her now. I'll make myself. She'll help me to." He took what rest he dared, and started up from it much later than he had intended, having had the talk with Lolita again in the room with the curtains. It was nine when he set out for the short-cut under the moon, dazed by his increasing torture. The brilliant disk, blurring to the eye, showed the mountains unearthly plain, beautiful, and tall in the night. By-and-by a mule fell and could not rise, and Genesmere decided it was as well for all to rest again. The next he knew it was blazing sunshine, and the sky at the same time bedded invisible in black clouds. And when his hand reached for a cloud that came bellying down to him, it changed into a pretzel, and salt burned in his mouth at the sight of it. He turned away and saw the hot, unshaded mountains wrinkled in the sun, glazed and shrunk, gullied like the parchment of an old man's throat; and then he saw a man in a steeple-hat. He could no more lay the spectre that wasted his mind than the thirst-demon which raged in his body. He shut his eyes, and then his arm was beating at something to keep it away. Pillowed on his saddle, he beat until he forgot. A blow at the corner of his eye brought him up sitting, and a raven jumped from his chest.

"You're not experienced," said Genesmere. "I'm not dead yet. But I'm obliged to you for being so enterprising. You've cleared my head. Quit that talk, Russ Genesmere." He went to the mule that had given out during the night. "Poor Jeff! We must lighten your pack. Now if that hunchback had died here, the birds would have done his business for him without help from any of your cats. Am I saying that, now, or only thinking it? I know I'm alone. I've travelled that way in this world. Why?" He turned his face, expecting some one to answer, and the answer came in a fierce voice: "Because you're a man, and can stand this world off by yourself. You look to no one." He suddenly took out the handkerchief and tore the photograph to scraps. "That's lightened my pack all it needs. Now for these boys, or they'll never make camp." He took what the mules carried, his merchandise, and hid it carefully between stones—for they had come near the mountain country—and, looking at the plain he was leaving, he saw a river. "Ha, ha!" he said, slyly; "you're not there, though. And

I'll prove it to you." He chose another direction, and saw another flowing river. "I was expecting you," he stated, quietly. "Don't bother me. I'm thirsty."

But presently as he journeyed he saw lying to his right a wide, fertile place, with fruit-trees and water everywhere. "Peaches too!" he sang out, and sprang off to run, but checked himself in five steps. "I don't seem able to stop your foolish talking," he said, "but you shall not chase around like that. You'll stay with me. I tell you that's a sham. Look at it." Obedient, he looked hard at it, and the cactus and rocks thrust through the watery image of the lake like two photographs on the same plate. He shouted with strangling triumph, and continued shouting until brier-roses along a brook and a farm-house unrolled to his left, and he ran half-way there, calling his mother's name. "Why, you fool, she's dead!" He looked slowly at his cut hands, for he had fallen among stones. "Dead, back in Kentucky, ever so long ago," he murmured, softly. "Didn't stay to see you get wicked." Then he grew stern again. "You've showed yourself up, and you can't tell land from water. You're going to let the boys take you straight. I don't trust you."

He started the mules, and caught hold of his horse's tail, and they set out in single file, held steady by their instinct, stumbling ahead for the water they knew among the mountains. Mules led, and the shouting man brought up the rear, clutching the white tail like a rudder, his feet sliding along through the stones. The country grew higher and rougher, and the peaks blazed in the hot sky; slate and sand and cactus below, gaping cracks and funnelled erosions above, rocks like monuments slanting up to the top pinnacles; supreme Arizona, stark and dead in space, like an extinct planet, flooded blind with eternal brightness. The perpetual dominating peaks caught Genesmere's attention. "Toll on!" he cried to them. "Toll on, you tall mountains. What do you care? Summer and winter, night and day, I've known you, and I've heard you all along. A man can't look but he sees you walling God's country from him, ringing away with your knell."

He must have been lying down during some time, for now he saw the full moon again, and his animals near him, and a fire blazing that himself had evidently built. The coffee-pot sat on it, red-hot and split open. He felt almost no suffering at all, but stronger than ever in his life, and he heard something somewhere screaming "Water! water! water!" fast and unceasing, like an alarm-clock. A rattling of stones made him turn, and there stood a few staring cattle. Instantly he sprang to his feet, and the screaming stopped. "Round 'em up, Russ Genesmere! It's getting late!" he yelled, and ran among the cattle, whirling his rope. They dodged weakly this way and that, and next he was on the white horse urging him after the cows, who ran in a circle. One struck the end of a log that stuck out from the fire, splintering the flames and embers, and Genesmere followed on the tottering horse through the sparks, swinging his rope and yelling in the full moon: "Round 'em up! round 'em up! Don't you want to make camp? All the rest of the herd's bedded down along with the ravens."

The white horse fell and threw him by the edge of a round hole, but he did not know it till he opened his eyes and it was light again, and the mountains still tolling. Then like a crash of cymbals the Tinaja beat into his recognition. He knew the slate rock; he saw the broken natural stairs. He plunged down them, arms forward like a diver's, and ground his forehead against the bottom. It was dry. His bloodshot eyes rolled once up round the sheer walls. Yes, it was the Tinaja, and his hands began to tear at the gravel. He flung himself to fresh places, fiercely grubbing with his heels, biting into the sand with his teeth; while above him in the cañon his placid animals lay round the real Tinaja Bonita, having slaked their thirst last night, in time, some thirty yards from where he now lay bleeding and fighting the dust in the dry twin hole.

He heard voices, and put his hands up to something round his head. He was now lying out in the light, with a cold bandage round his forehead, and a moist rag on his lips.

"Water!" He could just make the whisper.

But Lolita made a sign of silence.

"Water!" he gasped.

She shook her head, smiling, and moistened the rag. That must be all just now.

His eye sought and travelled, and stopped short, dilating; and Lolita screamed at his leap for the living well.

"Not yet! Not yet!" she said in terror, grappling with him. "Help! Luis!"

So this was their plot, the demon told him—to keep him from water! In a frenzy of strength he seized Lolita. "Proved! Proved!" he shouted, and struck his knife into her. She fell at once to the earth and lay calm, eyes wide open, breathing in the bright sun. He rushed to the water and plunged, swallowing and rolling.

Chapter VI

Luis ran up from the cows he was gathering, and when he saw what was done, sank by Lolita to support her. She pointed to the pool.

"He is killing himself!" she managed to say, and her head went lower.

"And I'll help you die, caberon! I'll tear your tongue. I'll—"

But Lolita, hearing Luis's terrible words, had raised a forbidding hand. She signed to leave her and bring Genesmere to her.

The distracted Luis went down the stone stairs to kill the American in spite of her, but the man's appearance stopped him. You could not raise a hand against one come to this. The water-drinking was done, and

Genesmere lay fainting, head and helpless arms on the lowest stone, body in the water. The Black Cross stood dry above. Luis heard Lolita's voice, and dragged Genesmere to the top as quickly as he could. She, seeing her lover, cried his name once and died; and Luis cast himself on the earth.

"Fool! fool!" he repeated, catching at the ground, where he lay for some while until a hand touched him. It was Genesmere.

"I'm seeing things pretty near straight now," the man said. "Come close. I can't talk well. Was—was that talk of yours, and singing—was that bluff?"

"God forgive me!" said poor Luis.

"You mean forgive me," said Genesmere. He lay looking at Lolita. "Close her eyes," he said. And Luis did so. Genesmere was plucking at his clothes, and the Mexican helped him draw out a handkerchief, which the lover unfolded like a treasure. "She used to look like this," he began. He felt and stopped. "Why, it's gone!" he said. He lay evidently seeking to remember where the picture had gone, and his eyes went to the hills whence no help came. Presently Luis heard him speaking, and, leaning to hear, made out that he was murmuring his own name, Russ, in the way Lolita had been used to say it. The boy sat speechless, and no thought stirred in his despair as he watched. The American moved over, and

put his arms round Lolita, Luis knowing
that he must not offer to help him do this.
He remained so long that the boy, who
would never be a boy again, bent over to
see. But it was only another fainting-fit.
Luis waited; now and then the animals
moved among the rocks. The sun crossed
the sky, bringing the many-colored evening,
and Arizona was no longer terrible, but
once more infinitely sad. Luis started, for
the American was looking at him and beck-
oning.

"She's not here," Genesmere said, dis-
tinctly.

Luis could not follow.

"Not here, I tell you." The lover touched
his sweetheart. "This is not her. My punishment is nothing," he went on, his face growing beautiful. "See there!"

Luis looked where he pointed.

"Don't you see her? Don't you see her
fixing that camp for me? We're going to
camp together now."

But these were visions alien to Luis, and
he stared helpless, anxious to do anything
that the man might desire. Genesmere's
face darkened wistfully.

"Am I not making camp?" he said.

Luis nodded to please him, without at all
comprehending.

"You don't see her." Reason was warring
with the departing spirit until the end.

"Well, maybe you're right. I never was sure. But I'm mortal tired of travelling alone. I hope—"

That was the end, and Russ Genesmere lay still beside his sweetheart. It was a black evening at the cabin, and a black day when Luis and old Ramon raised and fenced the wooden head-stone, with its two forlorn names.

HISTORICAL NOVELS
OF THE AMERICAN FRONTIERS

<u>DON WRIGHT</u>

☐	58991-2	THE CAPTIVES	$4.50
☐	58992-0		Canada $5.50
☐	58989-0	THE WOODSMAN	$3.95
☐	58990-4		Canada $4.95

<u>DOUGLAS C. JONES</u>

☐	58459-7	THE BAREFOOT BRIGADE	$4.50
☐	58460-0		Canada $5.50
☐	58457-0	ELKHORN TAVERN	$4.50
☐	58458-9		Canada $5.50
☐	58453-8	GONE THE DREAMS AND DANCING (Winner of the Golden Spur Award)	$3.95
☐	58454-6		Canada $4.95
☐	58450-3	SEASON OF YELLOW LEAF	$3.95
☐	58451-1		Canada $4.95

<u>EARL MURRAY</u>

☐	58596-8	HIGH FREEDOM	$4.95
☐	58597-6		Canada 5.95

Buy them at your local bookstore or use this handy coupon:
Clip and mail this page with your order.

Publishers Book and Audio Mailing Service
P.O. Box 120159, Staten Island, NY 10312-0004

Please send me the book(s) I have checked above. I am enclosing $_____
(please add $1.25 for the first book, and $.25 for each additional book to
cover postage and handling. Send check or money order only—no CODs.)

Name _____

Address _____

City _____ State/Zip _____

Please allow six weeks for delivery. Prices subject to change without notice.

MORE
HISTORICAL NOVELS
OF THE AMERICAN FRONTIERS

<u>JOHN BYRNE COOK</u>

THE SNOWBLIND MOON TRILOGY
(Winner of the Golden Spur Award)

☐	58150-4	BETWEEN THE WORLDS	$3.95
☐	58151-2		Canada $4.95
☐	58152-0	THE PIPE CARRIERS	$3.95
☐	58153-9		Canada $4.95
☐	58154-7	HOOP OF THE NATION	$3.95
☐	58155-5		Canada $4.95

<u>W. MICHAEL GEAR</u>

☐	58304-3	LONG RIDE HOME	$3.95
☐	58305-1		Canada $4.95

<u>JOHN A. SANDFORD</u>

☐	58843-6	SONG OF THE MEADOWLARK	$3.95
☐	58844-4		Canada $4.95

<u>JORY SHERMAN</u>

☐	58873-8	SONG OF THE CHEYENNE	$2.95
☐	58874-6		Canada $3.95
☐	58871-1	WINTER OF THE WOLF	$3.95
☐	58872-X		Canada $4.95

Buy them at your local bookstore or use this handy coupon:
Clip and mail this page with your order.

Publishers Book and Audio Mailing Service
P.O. Box 120159, Staten Island, NY 10312-0004

Please send me the book(s) I have checked above. I am enclosing $_____
(please add $1.25 for the first book, and $.25 for each additional book to
cover postage and handling. Send check or money order only — no CODs.)

Name _____

Address _____

City _____ State/Zip _____

Please allow six weeks for delivery. Prices subject to change without notice.

BESTSELLING BOOKS FROM TOR

THE BEST IN SUSPENSE